Life's
Short
Stories

Books by the Anonymous Author and Artist

Life's Mixed Poetry

Poems are mixed schematically, stylistically, and randomly.

Life's Novellas: Fate Waits Upon No One

The good and the bad are juxtaposed, chronologically, fictionally, and theatrically.

Their Poetic Minds

Poems are juxtaposed, religiously, femininely, and dichotomously.

Poems of Life

Poems are mixed schematically, stylistically, and randomly.

Life's Heart Break: A Novella

In the end, will Zenald discover what may be one of life's biggest heart-breaks: heart-ache?

Duty & Destruction I

A real female experiences life in and out of the U.S. military.

Life's Poetic Dichotomies

Some of life's biggest dichotomies are juxtaposed poetically.

Her Poetic Rise

It is for the religiously poetic that blends religion and feminism.

Art Book

The Diamond & Heart Art Collections

Pictures are exhibited, categorically, by coloring schemes and coloring mediums; all of which, have been affected with special effects.

Schemes: pastel shades; earth tones; primary colors; gray, black and white; black and white.

Mediums: colored pencils; water coloring; pastel coloring; acrylic coloring; oil coloring.

Life's
Short
Stories

Anonymous

Century Conquests

Life's Short Stories

Copyright © 2011 by Anonymous

www.centuryconquests.com
info@centuryconquests.com

ISBN: 978-0-9850698-3-4

Cover graphic designed by: Century Conquests © 2013

Century Conquests ® 2012

Life's

Short

Stories

Anonymous

Acknowledgements

For the small voice deep within me that now wants me to carry on fictionally.

I even thank every one who has helped with the publication of this book.

I thank, also, all the readers of my book, for permitting me the privilege; to entertain and enthrall you, as well as explain to you: my artistic, creative, and literary reasoning.

Author's Note

This is a work of fiction. In addition, and assuming no responsibility for any figurative or literal mix-up; best efforts have been put forth; to actualize the actuality of historical, cultural, social, and, religious, and, even, political, and the like; references, and, inferences, and even, interpretations, and so forth—or, forces, that are contained here in.

Additionally, the publisher and the author both have had no necessary need to denigrate any, ("so-called, or otherwise"), human figure; or, a company's product, or even, a company's service, and so on, except, in the case of actual necessity.

Table of Contents

Whether we fall by ambition, lust, or greed,
Like diamonds we are cut by our own dust.

—John Webster's: *The Duchess of Malfi*
(c. 1580—c. 1634)

Part I

I Need Not Be Down

Life has its problems, or ghosts.

On the surface, the old, dark, and weak man couldn't concentrate on his reading, most seemingly. Because, of the very ambivalent feelings that he was experiencing. He thus tossed the hackneyed book aside. Benjamin then scanned the dim-colored living room…, scanning too many reminders of his late wife, Idell. Next, Ben veered his position on the worn-out sofa and then eyed the antiquated piano. The sounds of Richard Rogers and Lorenz Hart's 1934—old and top hit—"Blue Moon," just, started echoing all through the shrinkingly small room. Ben only listened while Idell's beautifully old body of a ghost sat at the piano playing their favorite song. He just smiled and then settled back, some, on the well-worn settee.

A few minutes later, the music stopped. And, Ben just sat in roundly roaring silence.

All of a sudden, Ben grabbed the bible that he'd cast to the side and then threw it at the piano. "DAMN YOU!" he shrieked, soundly, or roundly, with grief. Plus, with a pretty petulant toss of his head, Ben raised his hands and then banged them right on the sofa—WHANG!

After having rushed right into the living room…, Zenobia roared, so roaringly, "Grandfather, what—"

"Please, just leave me in peace!"

"Peace? You're just throwin' things all around, what—oh my God—goodness…!" she cried, realizing, roundly, what was really going on; "She's gone…, and, forev'r! Or, Idell's dead…! But, we're not, and, if you're not goin' to continue livin'—well—"

Ben interposed—or, questioned, quite, grumpily, "Girl, haven't you any respect or decency…? Huh? Plus, shouldn't you be just tryin' to follow in *her* footsteps…?"

"What…? I've already told you—that, I've my *own* 'damn'd' life to live, 'without doubt or fail,' Grandfather—'you old grump….' I'm just about to—"

"Do what?"

"I'm goin' to bed," Zen stated, dryly, "since it's late…, good-night," turning right around and then disappearing, wordlessly, with a dry mouth.

It wasn't the right time or was it...? To face right down her grumpy grandfather that lived, seemingly, right, in the grumps, grumbling. And, who, almost, always, grumped, rather grumpily, about one thing or another thing or even some other thing.

Ben just sat on the worn-out sofa in the living room. He did so—long, after his only grandchild, or Zen had left the room. Then, he began tossing and turning, trying to find, presumably, a more comfortable position whence he sat. Of course, the ambiguity had re-visited him. Why wouldn't it...? Plus, Ben wanted or needed to do something about his ambivalence, possibly. Was he confused, scared, so lonely, or just plain mean, or even something else, to some extent? So, what was he to do about it all...? On the face of it, Ben was so tired, also, of the incredible strife, or the armed conflict between him and Zen. Such was why he probably chose not to grumble, anymore, for the time being, anyway.

...The music began, again, and the sure sounds of "Blue Moon" just echoed through out the room, living room. Was Ben now through living...? Has he now drowned completely—right, in a saltily sour sea of ghostly and immutable melancholy—or, super bitter-sweet sadness...? Just how sad was Ben, truly; seeing, at first, the darkness in his eyes, and the droopiness of his face—or, his gloomy expression. Oh...! How he just loved his wife's piano playing....

Ben fell asleep, eventually, on the circularly cozy couch with Idell's ghost of a lovingly warm, light, and bright body. Its luminosity lit up the dark room, ultimately, with warmth, and love, and even joy. It was lovely, too—secondly, seeing the joyful expression on Ben's face, snoring, at full volume.

The man was just irritating Zen..., at best, or worst, repulsing, if not repelling her. She'd to do something about it—soon. But, for the time being, Zen just had to keep her commitments.... So, she continued steering the old motor car right along an abandoned highway, so northerly, in the direction of Interstate-75, (or I-75). On this very cool, and, windy, and, even, seemingly shadowy Saturday—morning, in mid fall of 1979, the sun so glared. Right, in the bird-less and bluish-gray sky over grayish-black clouds while Chic's big musical hit "Good Times" played on the radio.

"Damnation...!" Zen lashed out. She looked briefly at the presumably lazy cows that sat right under some super shady trees. What Zen saw was an environment that she'd to just leave, soon, but, not—soon, enough. Her left hand grasped the steering wheel tighter; her heart began to palpitate; her dry mouth became crooked; she then banged her right tight fist against the car's dis-colored control-panel or dash-board. BANG…! Zen asked of no one, in particular, "…What damn good times…?" silencing the sounds of Chic's top song. "And, why the hell—I've been such a blithering fool…?"

For a second time, Zen looked around at the barren land and decrepit houses—or impoverishment. She just wanted or needed to leave it all behind, and, way. What was more, Zen so wanted to swallow her agony—or anger—irritation, but it wasn't that easy, at all. Zen's throat was still dry from her little or big run-in with Ben in the living room, last night. "Damn that man!" And, just, as she cursed a seemingly woeful widower, Zen realized that she'd passed her exit. "Goddamn him…!" She cursed Ben, yet again.

…Zen just spun the car right off the next exit of Interstate-75, (I-75). Then, she headed easterly toward Valdosta or a small, Georgian town about 40 miles north-east of Tallahassee, Florida. She thought, too, about Benjamin Zanuck or her grand-father; who was so fast becoming a real, if not an overly overt object of her true discontent, or her damnably dark disgruntlement. The maternal Black-Americans, or Ben and his dead wife—Idell, had raised their only grand-child—or, Zenobia—ever, since her natural parents died…, most tragically. Such happened in a terrible automobile accident some years ago. They did such, or raised her lovingly, Zen; yet—Ben, some-how, a bit too—damn, over-bearingly; or, so it always seemed to Zen, especially, since Idell's passing away, death.

Her late, paternal grand-mother's son or Zen's father was even over-bearing…, some-times. All, right, to what actual avail…? What about Zen's maternal mother or paternal grand-mother…? Zen just tried to remember far happier days: or, a time when her racially mixed parents were still alive, and, well; or, a time when she didn't care about being a cream-colored Mulatto, or penniless, or even powerless. The times were changing and she was changing right with the times, without doubt—or fail.

A fancy vehicle zoomed right by her, and Zen was brought right back to reality, and roundly.

As, her destination was close—but, not, nearly, close enough.

The once beautiful but now banal building stood away from the main road and faded in all its golden glory. The lush landscape that surrounded the once popular nursing home was now nothing more than unkempt vegetation. As time passed, the motor-cars that used to be parked in the gravel-leveled parking lot had all but disappeared. The nursing home served only as a pretty phantom, or a pretty pictogram of what so used to be. Just the same, still, that some families chose to use the old nursing home in lieu of the new nursing home, nearby.

Frankly, the nursing home's existence has been so dependent on the loyal business of such families or such citizens; otherwise, it stood to close its doors, perhaps, permanently, had those same folks—or, same citizens, or even, same families, so disappeared, as well. Needless, to say, that the super skeletal staff was very happy, also, about the left-over jobs or, so it seemed, indeed. YIPPEE! ...They all had yipped and yipped..., for days.

Zen had even wanted to work right at the nursing home. But, Ben had convinced her not to do it.... He instead persuaded Zen to just volunteer her services.... Zen believed whole-heartedly—that, it was because Ben feared—that, a real job meant some real independence, (or some *real freedom*), for her. Wasn't such a very good thing—right, along, with some privacy? Since such independence and freedom and even privacy, almost, always, has gone together.

In a so-called, private room on the second floor of the nursing home, the aged, frail, and gloomy—or, the African-American woman with salt-and-pepper-colored hair, just, waited. Georgina Lambert waited so impatiently for Zenobia Zella Zanuck to arrive. Meantime, Georgina just eyed the damnably dim-colored décor of her room. The low ceiling appeared to drop lower every single day. The low-priced curtains and old furniture—all, faded more with each passing day, even. Plus, the room's antiseptic smell only added to the room's utter unpleasantness. It was enough to make anyone just stop thinking about such.

She just looked at the utterly un-even and nakedly cold tiling on the floor. Georgina was about to crawl from her uncomfortably high bed. Then, she uttered under her breath..., "maybe later...," and twirling back—over, to the left side of the bed. Georgina just frowned and then lowered her head: all coiled up. Was Ben keeping Zen...? How many times had Georgina tried to talk to Ben...? She'd tried talking to him only too many times..., or, so it seemed to Georgina, and, needless to say, to Zen. Georgina frowned, once, again, lowered her head, and then shook it from side to side. Where was Zen? Georgina just twirled back, over, to the right side of the bed.

Zen drove the old motor car over the circularly cracked path that led right to Sunshine Nursing Home and Rehabilitation Center. In no time, at all, she secured a parking space in its very holey parking lot. The motor of Ben's old motor-car was thus quieted. Never mind securing it, for there was hardly anything to secure.... Beamingly, Zen just slid out of the car. She truly loved working, or, more precisely, so volunteering, right, at the nursing home. Zen made haste—not, to waste any more time, precious time. She walked hastily along the walk way that led right to the big, double-wide, plus, welcoming door of the nursing home of a rehabilitation center.

Inside of Sunshine Nursing Home, Zen was greeted—or, bombarded, smilingly, if not grinningly, and pryingly, right, by a middle-aged, portly, and crinkly nurse-aid with slant eyes: "How ya doin'? …I didn't see ya last week. Here for ya weekly visit…?" so pried the nurse of an aid with an abundantly Asian accent.

Hastening to the elevator in the bare lobby, Zen only shook her head in agreement and waved hello and then good-bye, for now. For sure, the two planned to talk about nothing, in particular. It was just plainly un-avoidable in the ghostly rehabilitation center of a nursing home. Zen and her patient— or good friend of a very dear mentor, contrarily, had lots to chat or talk about, in particular.

"Okey-doke, we'll chit-chat…, later, Dearie," the nurse-aid retreated. Fortunately, or unfortunately, for her, there was work that just needed to be done.

The elevator hastened Zen right to the second floor. Afterwards, she stepped on, speedily, and stepping right to Georgina's room of a temporary home. Since, Zen didn't appreciate any amount of lateness. For, punctuality meant something to her—right, along, with her thoughts, words, and ways, almost, always. But, what were the truly important words that Zen very much wanted or needed to hear or even say, at least, to some extent?

WHOOSH…! Some male orderly whooshed right by Zen in the hall way en route to her sought-after or desirable destination.

Neither could Zen help beaming at him, and speaking, spontaneously, "Hi, and have a 'damn' good day."

Looking back over his right shoulder, "Thanks, and the same right to you," reciprocated the apparently industrious male with stretched, hurried, or calculated steps: right, in a pair of very brand new-looking sneakers.

A soft knock was heard at the door, "Come in," Georgina said.

Beamingly, Zen walked right into the room, and speaking—inquiring: "Hello Mrs. Lambert, and how you're doing?"

Having snapped a very pretty photograph of Zen right with her eyes' agedly photographic lens, she answered: "My Dear, you just brighten up the day and my sight, or life. Oh! I feel good now that—"

Zen interjected, "You look good—or, wonderful, your-self," and then sat down in a chair next to the bed where Georgina was lying. Did she really look wonderful? In reality, it didn't matter. Because, such thought and like-minded thoughts were what mattered most: politeness, kindness, generosity, and a sense of humor, and even respect, or self-respect.

Georgina just initiated the discourse…, "How've you been…, truly?" Storing the pretty photo of her dear friend or mentee—Zen, in the store house of her circularly curious mind.

Momentarily, Zen just wanted to deceive Georgina but she couldn't, didn't. "It's my grandfather"—she stopped abruptly and then looked away…. Zen even lowered her head, shaking it, loathingly.

"What about him…? And, please look at me…!" questioned, and then demanded Georgina; who then sat right up in the curative or therapeutic and unseemly but necessary yet repellant or debatably hospitable bed.

"I'm just about finished or through listenin' to Benjamin's overly out-dated beliefs—'or, philosophy of life and methodology of livin' it—life—my damn life!'"

Waiting for the inevitable words to come that weren't warmed-over—but, instead, chilly, or cold; Georgina sat frozen, and, quite.

Sure, enough, the heated words came…, heatedly, if not, explosively, and un-freezing Georgina: "I'll be damn'd if allow that man of an oppressor, 'digressor, regressor, repressor, and so on—depressor,' or my grandfather to continue poisonin' my mind—me, 'or my damn life! No goddamn more…!'" Zen swore, or exploded, and then banging her super-tight and left fist on her pocketbook. She then put the hurt pocketbook down, on the dull deck aside her. "NO WAY…!" Zen again exploded and then looked imploded, frankly.

Settling down, some, Zen continued, on:

> No, Sirree…! Mrs. Lambert, I know that you and my
> grandfather have been friends for a long time, 'supposedly.'
> My grandmother even considered you as her dear sister. And,
> I should speak more kindly of Ben considerin' all that he's
> done for me. But, I'm 'bout through listenin' to his overly
> out-dated beliefs, or opinions, or even point-of-view…!

Zen swore, again, and then raising her hands well above her head in irritation, or definite disgust.

"Settle down, Dear…."

Irritatingly, Zen just cross-questioned her friend of a prized mentor…, "Settle down?"

"Yes—well, I understand your loathsome pain and that you're very much irritated…. I've talked and talked to Ben…, but it just hasn't done any good. Still, I support you—"

"Oh! Thank you, Mrs. Lambert! And, I plan to make my move, soon, 'but, not nearly, soon—enough!'"

"Oh?"

"Yes Ma'am, I certainly am…."

"I see…, Dearie," Georgina so commented, and comprehending Zen's plight, assumably, to some extent, if not a great extent.

Rising and shining…, "As far as I'm concerned," Zen told Georgina, "the pretty poisonous price of persecution for us—or, females, still has to be paid, and, most prettily. 'Likewise, I shall pay my damn just or fair share or even die tryin', without doubt or fail…! Steady.'" Twirling, about, "I've been blessed, as well. Since, my parents were wise, enough, having left me a trust account, though, modest." She started pacing back and forth, suddenly, right, in the center of the soundly shrinkable room. "The money's stood, so solidly, or readily, and rightly, to just fulfill some of my deliciously good dreams— 'or, my full potential,'" added Zen.

One of Georgina's big regrets in life was that she and her deceased husband, or George never had any children. She'd so pledged that if she were ever given a real chance to affect or effect a young person's life, especially, a young female's life—then, she'd to do just that; So, Georgina interpolated: "Yes…! Fulfill your dreams…, my Dear!"

Right, in a pair of old loafers, Zen smiled, standing taller, and feeling stronger, and even looking eagle-eyed, right now, as opposed to see-sawing: or, zig-zagging—so wig-wagging: moving, up, down, and all around, almost, certainly, purposelessly. Yet, she'd a purpose. It was a damn good thing, too: that, Zen had read several books, so purposely, or, on purpose, about Realism and all of its nakedly nasty nitty-gritty…; or, more, to the point, she read some of the very beloved books by the marvelous masters of urban or black literature: Donald Goines, and, Robert Beck—(or, Iceberg Slim). Such was intended to help Zen deal, roundly, and forcefully, with the real world….

Georgina began coughing.

Zen offered, "Do you care for a glass of water or something—"

"Yes!"—Georgina gasped.

Zen scurried, purposefully, right, to the room's downright diminutive dinette. She then returned in such record-breaking time with that drink for Georgina, who now looked a tad pale.

Georgina reciprocated, "Thank you, Dearie," and then drinking a long swallow of the fresh water.

It wasn't just like a bolt out of the bluish-gray yonder, either, when Zen announced or spoke, further: "You're most welcome. Also, I'm getting a real job, buying a new car, and going to college—or travel. Plus, with some luck, I'll buy a new home, 'or my *own* damn home.' God help him—or, Ben, if he even thinks about trying to stand in the way of my impending quest, or success—"

"What then?" Georgina interjected, questioningly. She even put down her drink on the bed stand next to the bed. Georgina waited, as well, for some more chilly, or cold, or heated words to gush heatedly, if not cold-bloodedly from Zen's mouth.

She just breathed hard and then replied, "Well, haw—let's just hope 'or pray' that he doesn't…. 'Steady now…!'" A wildly wide smile stretched right across Zen's face, "Don't worry, Mrs. Lambert…, and thanks again for believing in me. I love you—" she started to say, rather dotingly.

"I love you…, too, Darlin'," responded Georgina, lovingly, and, right, with utterly unfailing support.

"So, what else can I get you or do for you, my most solid supporter?"

Georgina re-acted, or responded, pointing…, "Well, those flowers on the dresser could or can sure use some more fresh water—or, even, a little or a big human touch—"

"All right—in fact, I'll just do the usual…, tidy up. Then, you'll get your beauty-treatment. Afterwards, a game of Solitaire will be in order…."

Georgina snapped another pretty picture of the pretty industrious and nineteen-year-old female with thickly golden-brown and medium-length hair; whose wide waves flowed so freely about Zen's perfectly round face; whose fantastically fine features appeared chiseled. "Thank you, once again," spoke Georgina, lovingly, and now glimpsing at Zen's beautifully dark-brown eyes, face; whose raised cheek-bones sat, so roundly, and superbly, amid a narrow nose and laborious lips. They were lips that aimed, so absolutely, to speak the truth—soon; but, how, soon…? Time was definitely of the essence. Since, it always ticked away and waited on no one; who sought so uncertainly to free oneself from some terribly tight spot.

"You're quite welcome…!" Zen proclaimed, or declared, again; then, moving her petite yet firm and shapely frame—or body, so industriously, in a dark denim, out-fit; "Don't worry…, either," tidying up, "since I'll succeed, without doubt—fail! I've lots of hope, faith, and ambition, and even strength, or staying power—*personal power*. 'Folks are finished standing in the way of my quest for success—damn'd, though it may very well be….'"

There was neither time nor place nor space for any second or third or even fourth thoughts…, utter un-steadiness: or see-sawing—and zig-zagging, damn wig-wagging. Zen had better stay super strong…. Needless, to say, that a cool drink of some fresh water helped; so, rightly, to wet the dryness of her declarations, or proclamations—dry mouth. Right, in the midst of tending to Mrs. Lambert's wants and needs, Zen so managed to flavor if not savor some fresh water, herself.

The two, and dear, and even devoted friends, un-likely, though they might've been, went right on to enjoy each other's company. In other words, an enjoyable morning or day, it all had turned right out to be.

Ben just sat on the haunting bed. His teary eyes poured over the dark, cold, and very empty room. Memories engulfed him, eyeing the old wooden furniture. That Idell had spent many of days and nights shining, so faithfully, with Old English, furniture polish. He looked at the dresser's mirror and even saw Idell's lovingly warm reflection—or, an absolute apparition. Ben smiled, half-heartedly, and then his eyes settled on a bunch of starkly fake flowers…; which sat in a dreadfully dusty vase on the dresser, to the side.

He inhaled deeply and smelled the super sweet scent of his wife's, or Idell's favorite flowers…, Acacia Blossoms. The hauntingly sweet-smelling flowers just infused the once oppressive or airless air. Smiling and turning around, Ben felt the smoothness of one of Idell's hands on his left shoulder; yet, he didn't see her…. His rough hands then clutched, rather, circularly, the cuddly cover that lay on the big, old, and lumpy bed. Ben just squeezed and squeezed it, squeezing life right back into the starkly naked blanket. A super sentimental spirit was taking him right over.

Quite un-aware that he was doing so, Ben took a little photograph of Idell from his wallet…. "You'd been a roundly remarkable woman, Darlin'," purred Ben. "Why did you've to leave me…?" He questioned the photo for the umpteenth time. "You'd be pretty proud of her…, Hun. Because, Zen has turned out, well, except"—Ben halted, very hastily, and then carried on with very watery eyes…: "Maybe, she thinks that I'm just too damn hard on her—but, it's for the best…," he purported with lovingly teary eyes. Ben brought the aged memento—or, photo much closer to his face.

Carrying on, "I've only tried to instill in Zen the values that you and I've treasured, so dearly. She and I or we'll always be together, and Zen will never leave me, with any luck," spoke Ben, gloomily, if not grumpily. Next, he whispered, to Idell's little photograph, "Oh how I love—and, miss you so, Darlin'." Ben then kissed it, kissing the warm, bright, and, light photo of a dotingly deceased woman of a ghost…. Ben put the picture of Idell back in his wallet, eventually, and, with great care.

He then sauntered over to the dresser's mirror. Seeing that his tie was crooked, Ben straightened it, up, atop his old yet crisp and white shirt. He even wanted to put on a very different suit. Because, Idell never liked the suit that Ben was wearing, not, at all. Of course, she'd her reasons for not liking it. And, Ben just didn't like thinking about such. The suit had cost too damn much according to Idell; that, such money should've been spent on.... "I've time to change into another suit...," Ben blurted, and unbuttoning his jacket; "I'll wear my Sunday best—or, Idell's favorite suit...."

She would've been dressed for church ordinarily; instead, Zen wanted only to be left to her own vices: dressed casually comfortable in an old house coat—and, some old house slippers; plus, her hair was even full of some old rollers or some old curlers. She'd found it, still, within her person to perform the morning ritual, or prepare Ben's breakfast. Now, Zen peered through the open curtain of the small window. Was she wondering about Ben's response to her brand spanking new news...? She also wanted to yell out...: Hurry up, Old Man...! But, Zen just waited, most impatiently.

He was through moseying about or so it seemed. Since, the appealing aroma of the fantastically fresh coffee, syrupy pancakes, and countrified ham propelled Ben to accelerate his steps. He just left the bed room behind and then strutted down the hall, then through the house, en route.

Still, strutting, to some extent, right, into the kitchen..., "Why aren't you dressed for church?" inquired Ben.

Zen just shriveled for a moment or two. Her young heart skipped one or two or even three beats, possibly. She then released the curtain. "Hum— I'm not feelin' well," Zen fibbed, some-what, and stepping unsteadily toward the stove, in the small kitchen of the small house of a super suffocative home.

Ben sat at the kitchen table whilst Zen served him, breakfast.

"How're you this mornin', Grandfather? 'Steady.'"

He answered—cross-examined, "I'm fine, and what's ailin' you?"

Zen just put Ben's pre-made yet hot cup of coffee right on the table, unshakably. "Grandfather, I'm gettin' a real job, 'or leavin'...,'" she asserted, so dryly, and steadily.

His old heart skipped one or two or even three beats, quite, possibly. "Uh...? What'd you say...?" Ben asked and wished, most probably, that he'd misunderstood Zen.

"'Steady, now…!' Listen, Grandfather, I've meditated on this choice and—"

"I needn't—or, won't hear of it…!"

Zen just stood with nerves made of pretty, pitch-black steel. Then, she spoke, soundly, or roundly, and very resolutely: "…Your love's dangerous—'or, poisonous!' It's just too 'damn' smothery! And, it's un-rightly preventin' me from becomin' the Renaissance woman that I ought to become. 'But, no goddamn more…!'"

She just wanted or needed to be some other place, or else where. Zen decided, too, to use her last ammunition to authenticate—if not, to fire up her case: or, her nakedly noble cause: "Pretty please, just don't let what I've said enter one ear and then exit, 'very easily,' out the other ear. I'm 19-years-old, smart, strong, and life's just waitin' for me to conquer it, rather, forcefully. 'And, I shall do it, without doubt, or fail…! Since, I intend to out-play, out-work, and out-last—all, that would even try to out-distance me!'" She carried on, boldly—bravely: "I'm now takin' control of my *own* life, or destiny…!" GOOD! Her sense of self-worth or confidence was right in tact, now, among other things.

Ben just ate his food with a measure of glee-less gluttony in an effort to avoid the utterly un-speak-able matter, or conversation.

"Grandfather please, for we've to just talk about this 'and we shall, without fail…,'" pleaded Zen, so forwardly; "I'm so sorry—but, the time has just come—"

…More than just poker-faced and grumpy but even roundly or utterly un-receptive, he interjected—or, scolded her, sternly: "To turn your back on me and every darn thing that I've taught or given you?" and then swallowing a lengthy swallow of the scorching or very hot coffee.

"Taught? It's been more like burdened! Plus, your lessons are a great hardship for me if you want or need to know the truth! 'Or, the whole truth and nothin' but the goddamn'd truth!'" Zen informed Ben, most passionately. Neither, did she flinch one single bit, nor shrivel up…. Now wasn't the time to just wither away on some seemingly and darkly gray day that wanted only to stand or stay in her way: No goddamned way…!

Ben didn't care for this female of a grand-daughter that had changed, over night, on the face of it, so to speak. In no time, at all, Ben rose whence he sat, trembling, some. "Excuse me. But, church is where I'm now headed. What's more, I'll just ask God to forgive—or, to help you…," Ben told Zen, grumpily, and, quite glaringly.

She questioned, heatedly, "Forgive me for what…?"

He just stated, frostily, and, very, "Because, you're a malingerer—or, a time-waster," and then doing an about-face, frigidly, before disappearing.

Ostensibly, Ben wanted or needed Zen to be more like Idell—but, to what real avail? Did the thought even cross his mind that Zen could fail…?

Zen's deceased parents, or Zack and Zelma Zanuck both had labored right at their farm business until their utterly unfortunate death…. They had stipulated further in their Last Will of Testament, in the event of their deaths, to liquidate the business, among other assets: life insurance, retirement funds, and so forth. In which case, Ben and Idell both—or the lawful guardians were to use the money to assist in Zen's rearing…. In addition, some money had been placed into a trust account or a trust fund for Zen; who believed such to be, at least, $65,000.00.

Ben had inculcated, also, in Zen's mind that she should never touch the money—but, for, in the case of a true emergency…. Didn't he fathom the urgency of Zen's plight, to just get on with her life…? Since, she was tired, and, terribly, of all the damn strife…. Ben had even emphasized repeatedly to Zen: You've a home, already, living with me; an honorable life, (or volunteer work); a car to take you to and fro, (or his old car); a life-long friend, (Mrs. Lambert), most, supposedly; and, you've even me to look after you…, quite, definitely; but, to what actual avail…?

Now, Ben was having second or even third thoughts about his very adamant position, or, so it seemed. Nor was it surprising. That, a religiously, if not, a conscientiously self-confessed man such as he would seek, soundly, or roundly, some un-colorful or colorful consolation: or even guidance, from his Master. Just, tossing and turning on the long and wooden bench of a seat of the front row of the small yet welcomingly fathom-less room—or, church; Ben searched it for a circularly certain clue.

Was he feeling very different or more open if not hassle-free or even stress-free? Was the stress that he felt earlier concerning his roundly riotous run-in with Zen, so dissipating? Did Ben really want to abate the matter—or, what, exactly…? It appeared that his breathing slowed down, and his heart pulsated in very soft vibrations. Did Ben feel lighter…, and, much? Was his mind now opening up, more? "Oh help me, God, please!" Ben implored his Savior and then knelled on stiffly bent knees. He lowered his head, folded his hands together, and then spoke rather sincerely:

> Dear Father, I've so tried to do right by Zen. I've even tried to school her accordin' to Idell's—or your principles. What good has it done? I've given to her, when I didn't have any thing to give. Still, she wants more of everything. I've taken her places

but no place is ever good enough. God, ahhh, it's Gina—or, Georgina. That woman has some kind of dark power over my grand-baby! She's been fillin' Zen's head with so many fancy ideas. Now, ahhhh—you know, that I do respect Gina, well, nowadays, I've little respect for her.... Why God would that woman just turn my grand-child against me? And, what am I do about it all? Huh? Please tell—or, help me...! PRETTY, PLEASE!

After a minute or two, a soft yet strong but unusual and authoritative or superior voice stated, or more accurately, ordered: "Let her go."

"What?"

"Let her go...! For, it's far easier to hold on than it is to let go..., my Son, Child. And, what will you gain if you just continue to suffocate or stifle Zen's high hopes, or delicious dreams? Give her some liberty or time alone—autonomy."

"What'll I gain...? I've nothin' to gain"—Ben stopped—all, at once, and, quite searchingly.

Did he realize finally—just, how wrong he'd been...? Ben assented to that circularly commanding voice: "Please, or pretty please, just, forgive me, Father, for I've sinned, badly." Most, conceivably, such compunction rose up inside Ben, realizing with some measure of clarity: the absolutely awful truth of the matter. He just stood right—up, and then looked right—upward, then swallowed right—hard. Because, Ben now knew, exactly, what he'd to do...: He just had to make amends without doubt—or, fail!

Hence, it was a superlatively late and Sunday afternoon or even early evening seen very rarely by Zen. The fallen sun just collided, and colorfully, if not fantastically, right with the very bluish-yellow horizon, whilst pinkish-white-colored clouds just floated about. In the distance, some lively trees just rocked back and forth. They even suffused a super sugary smell in the air. Its sweetness or freshness gave Zen a sense of spanking brand new hope, faith, and ambition, and even strength: or staying power, if not *personal power*.

It was some sight, too, of Ben's old motor-car cruising right down the road leading to their home of a very soon-to-be, liberal house. He drove into the driveway. Ben even saw Zen as she rose right from a deck chair on the front porch of the house, or, their house; but, not, for much longer..., quite, presumably.

He exited the vehicle and then started lagging right toward her. Then, if on cue, Ben picked up his pace in a real effort to win the race; as, he'd to just let Zen go, first; and, just, as he's since been told by his Master, without doubt—or fail.

Ben just gazed at Zen's dark-brown eyes, gleaming, as though they belonged to a once young Idell. The exquisiteness of Zen's features caused him to freeze, fundamentally. He was hypnotized, so hauntingly, if not frozen right by her—Zen, and, not Idell, and, not this time. Ben came right back to the real world, since; or, was it time, actually, for some reality: his and Zen's actuality…?

She queried, "Grandfather, you're all right…?" Then, Zen suggested, "Why don't you just have a seat outside before goin' in…."

Pretty, un-puzzled, Ben sat in a deck chair on the front porch. Next, Zen sat adjacently to him in another deck chair—"Grandfather, pretty please, just hear me out…!" begged Zen.

Ben retained or maintained his very new-found composure, gathering his thoughts, carefully, and, very: "I'd just like to speak…, first, please," he requested, rather smilingly.

"Okay."

"Please, forgive me. For, I've been a selfishly old man or, a fantastic, if not, a fabulous fool—but, no damn more! The way that I've been tryin' to hold on to you, or hold you back, or even take you down and all…. It's just plain wrong—WRONG! But, no goddamn more…!"

"Now, may I speak?"

"Yes, of course."

Eyeing her grandfather, warm-heartedly, Zen spoke her true heart:

> I'll always be your lovin' grand-daughter. Plus, I'm grateful, truly, that you've taken care of me so well 'although, most over-bearingly.' I know, as well, that you're scared if I were to leave—that, I'll never return, or, if so, hardly ever. You, also, think, that once I start to spend *my money*—that, I'll be too 'damn' good for you. I'll never be that way—ever!

She paused, very briefly, and then continued right on, so smartly, and courageously: "I just feel like I'm dyin' inside…! Grandfather, I need not—or, I will not be oppressed any longer, 'nev'r, again…! EV'R!' *I need not be down*, 'quite simply.'"

Ben hugged Zen, caringly, or, most lovingly, and, in doing so, he was more able to let go than ever before…. "You've such potential…. So, just pursue your dreams or deliciously good dreams!" he exclaimed, beamingly, and, rather un-begrudgingly. It wasn't the time to neither begrudge nor be an old grumpy grump, living in the grumps, grumbling, most grumpily. Besides, it was much easier to hold on…, than it was to let go; now, very contrarily, it was so damn easy just letting go…. Ben's Master had even told him such—Proverbs 3, 5-6: "Trust in the Lord with all your heart and lean not on your own understanding; in all your ways acknowledge him, and he will direct your paths."

"Thank you…!" Zen exclaimed, reciprocating, and roundly. Next, she smiled inwardly and then outwardly if not quite proudly.

It was at such moment, more than likely, that Zenobia Zella Zanuck realized something significant—at last: By standing her ground, and fighting to be free to live her *own* life, such didn't necessarily sway Benjamin Zanuck to her side; but, instead, it swayed, or better yet, it solidified her own self-will or absolute ambition. Also, without doubt or fail, she just aimed to pursue her own aims—or, very good wishes, dreams. That, it was how, often-times, the awfully bitter-sweet cup-cake of life crumpled—or, crumbled: crumpling, or crumbling right into bits and pieces; and, having done so, long, before such degeneration was re-generated back into a super sweet whole, again.

It was very practical that a great measure of peace ensued pertaining to the two; or the one free, and the other just beginning to feel free. God had known it, without a doubt: some pretty possible peace ensuing…. Such was most evident in *Reinhold Niebuhr's* (1892-1971) "The Serenity Prayer." By chance, or, by design, did Ben remember it: "The Serenity Prayer?" If so, had it been some sort of real reinforcement? To just let his grand-daughter loose without delay, into the damnably dark, deep, and dirty, and even deleterious, or dangerous jungle of a world? That has been the utter under-belly. That, the utterly un-mistakable masters of black or urban literature: Robert Beck—(or, Iceberg Slim, 1918-1992); and, Donald Goines (1936-1974)—both, had thus spoken all about…?

Part II

Growing Young

Has age been only a number?

The suburban address addressed several things that surely facilitated one's well-being, and state of mind, if not peace of mind. *Fae Festa* was a very imposing and five-acre estate; which was nestled, quite nicely, amid an autumnal landscape and located on the outskirts of Suffolk, Virginia. Inside the ten-feet and cemented gate, and, to the right was a horse-riding trail; plus, a stable that housed three beautifully colored horses: snow-white, charcoal-grey, plus reddish-brown. To the mansion's left was a Jacuzzi enclosed in a near Olympic-sized swimming pool; whose sapphire-colored water glittered, just, like diamonds beneath the sun-light. Near the pool were a jogging track, and a callisthenic course, all of which had been useless, lately.

The mansion had some rooms, moreover, that were complementary, and, circularly, for one's health: steamy sauna, dry sauna, mentholated room, whirlpool, and an exercise room, gym. As of late, not only had those physical objects that so served to complement one's well-being been abandoned; but, also, they'd begun to haunt the mistress of the mansion in a bad way. There was some old-styled and mahogany-colored furniture on the second floor of the huge house inside the big bedroom. It'd been imported from *Bonn, West Germany*, for a very special occasion. The two colorfully and imaginatively impressionistic paintings...; both of which just hung on the bedroom's walls, had been bought, as well, for a unique occasion in *Toulouse, France*; none of which held their special meaning, any longer.

The room's décor, once the circularly colorful color of love and life; just, so very inviting and soothing in its affect and its effect both, have all but disappeared.... The woman or mistress of the magnificent mansion even felt that all the good in her life, or peace—sanity; attitude—mood; health—vigor; love—affection; happiness—joy; and, success—victory; and, even, beauty—spirituality; have all but gone away—stray, too. Not, surprising, that Mable Maddox just tossed and turned in the love-less and king-sized bed.

She awoke in a nick of time..., to get a damnably dark peek of a man; who, Mable had just begun to look down on, or, so loathe. Saul Maddox was stepping, un-steadily, from their bedroom—or, better, the bedroom, en route: to his roomy home-office, as usual. Her eyes settled on the left side of the bed where Saul's un-steady head had rested. Was rest, or better yet, serenity, for those who slept, serenely, only? Mable then leaned over, to his side of the bed. She wanted or needed to feel the emotions once associated with utterly unadulterated love and utterly unadulterated loyalty.

As if on cue, Mable recoiled, coiling right—up. She was so weakened if not sickened by downright disenchantment. Looking at that one dent in the silken linen, Mable just frowned and then swallowed her disillusionment, or ill feeling. She also needed to get out of the bed. But, thus far, Mable hadn't found the ambition to rise from the miserably immeasurable ditch or trench whence she'd fallen. Every single time that she thought about her husband's; or, thought about Saul's nakedly or damnably dark debauchery, a super thick cloud of disappointment descended right on her…: like, a hungrily poisonous predator devouring its prey, and most unmercifully. Mable was flattened, and defeated, if not devoured, right, by the heavy weight of downright discontent, all over again: or, by her husband's starkly dark depravity.

Right, before Mable rose from the bed, she shrieked, soundly, "Damn you…!" banging a right tight fist on Saul's pillow and flattening it…; "How could you…?" she so questioned Saul's ghostly impression of a dent. Steady. Mable glanced at the digital clock that just sat on her night stand, realizing that she needed to get up, now. Or, produce. So, Mable sat up-right and then tossed her legs out of the bed. She was about to rise when the photograph of her and Saul, which sat right on the night-stand, too, so grabbed her attention. His deviously debauched grin just added insult to injury—or, pain. Nor could Mable help to question the under-lying motives that led to her husband's wild waywardness or nasty naughtiness.

Was his circularly corporeal affinity for the other woman, or another woman more than just physical? Was it at least psychological if not spiritual in some meaningfully small way? When, exactly, did the genuine gaiety and pure passion just vanish from their own relationship, or so-called marriage? Or, more precisely, was there ever any to begin with—passionately stead-fast love? Again, Mable just recoiled, and rolling her eyes away from the photo, downwardly. A very disdainful look of damnably dark disdain played across her semi-aged face, countenance. Mable was pained as if she'd been maimed, grimacing, grotesquely.

Turning the picture's frame, down, on the night stand, Mable tried to dismiss all thoughts of Saul. Success had once been a big part of Mable's big game-plan. She just never wanted to be tamed, or be taken down by some let-down, or even some life-sized let-down. She was just no downer, supposedly, tolerating some come-down. Mable rose from the bed, consequently: and, her head held high; her body erect; her dignity, somewhat, in tact. Steady now…! She even managed to mosey on, right, to her private bathroom. Afterwards, Mable ended up on the terrace of a super spacious sanctuary.

The terrace over looked much of the left side of the estate, including the swimming pool, and jogging track, and even a finely cultivated garden of very tamed wild flowers; whose range of colors were a colorful mixture of yellowish-lavender, winsome-pink, and forest-green. There were the Indian Paintbrush (*Castilleja coccinea)*; Meadow Beauty (*Rhexia aristosa*); plus, Marsh Marigold, (*Caltha palustris*), among other wild flowers. On the terrace were three sets of the same furniture: or, two flowerily vibrant chaises; plus, three patio tables adorned with vibrantly flowery and circularly cushy chairs, that sat right under widely open umbrellas; all of which were complemented, circularly, right, by little bouquets of poisonous *Harlequin Lupines* (*Lupinus stiversii[es]*); which sat quite poisonously on the crystal-like patio tables.

How ironic Mable thought—that such gorgeous flowers, or *Harlequin Lupines*; whose lavender, yellow, plus crimson color coupled with its satiny feel and honeyed scent concealed its nastily dark poison…. Mable pushed the vase of flowers—aside. For, a serious frown, if not a serious scowl appeared on her face, frowning, and then scowling, or glowering, and grotesquely. The plants were Saul's most favorite flowers. And, just, the very simple thought of anything associated with him; or, that so-called man of a husband; or, that dreadfully malignant male—well, served only to repulse, or rather pointedly, to repel Mable in a darkly bad way.

The middle-aged and portly yet pretty productive house-keeper was pleased, most probably. That Mable had risen, finally, right, from her bed of a refuge. She wanted if not needed to get her boss's or, Mable's bedroom in its proper order before the morning was over. *Cianna* or the Hispanic house-keeper wanted or needed, as well, to get her boss-lady on her way: so rightly, to greet and then conquer a brand spanking new day…. More than likely, it appeared, right, to *Cianna*, that Mable's spirits had been spiraling downward, or way downhill; and, to what actual avail…? Carefully climbing the widely winding staircase, *Cianna* made her way from down stairs to up stairs, or, to the terrace—first; where upon she greeted Mable with a so-called stimulant, or a shot-in-the-arm, or even a pick-me-upper.

Cianna just approached her, "Good mornin', Madam," spoke *Cianna*, handing Mable some hot herb tea, "and, how're you, this mornin'?"

Mable responded—or, reciprocated, "Morning. I'm fine…, and thank you…," and then reaching for the pretty porcelaneous cup and saucer: or, a colorfully flora set of richly inherited dishware.

"You look radiant," *Cianna* added; "so, you're all dressed and ready for your mornin' swim—or work-out—GOOD…!"

…Mable just flavored or savored a super stretched-out swallow of the herb tea and then placed it right on the patio table. "Yes—that I am. And, I'm even grateful for my heated swimming pool..., 'which will belong, solely, to me...,'" Mable elaborated. What was Mable now planning to do...? Huh?

Cianna exclaimed—or, proclaimed, observing the very dim glimmer in Mable's olive-colored eyes: "That's great...! Since, you don't want to let yourself go—or, ignore your health for too long."

Mable stated, and, almost, nonchalantly, "Thank you, *Cianna*. Also, I'll take my brunch right out here on the terrace," looking at the sporty, scuba diver's watch that was on her left wrist; "in about—ahhh—an hour or so."

She acknowledged the request..., "Don't worry, Madam, because I've somethin' that's special, and planned, especially, for you."

Mable just remarked, and picking up her cup of tea that was set aside: "You're so very kind. I thank you.... 'And, if only that would-be or so-called husband of mine could be more like you instead of quite un-kind. Damn that weak and foolish man—or, damned male peon of a philanderer...!'"

"Really, it's nothin'.... I'm just so happy to see you up and about..., again," said *Cianna*, and patting her boss on the shoulder, most smilingly.

Cianna turned on her heels and then disappeared. Mable was pleased, too, that the some-times over-protective house-keeper didn't pry; or, that, she didn't question her about her recent despondency, which was obvious, most likely. Mable inhaled the sweetness of the fruit and almond, herb tea; whose ingredients were cinnamon, orange peel, rose hips, rooted carob, and hibiscus flowers, and even roasted chicory root; all of which just reminded Mable, and roundly, of her love of unaffectedness or naturalness.

Mable's attitude about artlessness, as of late, just, oscillated back and forth. Because, of the seemingly evil seed that Saul had since inculcated in her mind's eye or memory. Did he want that one seed to just take root; or, to just implant itself at the innermost part of Mable's soul; then, to just bloom in all its damnably dark or black glory...? She savored or flavored another long swallow of the herb tea and then put it to the side. Next, Mable looked over the terrace, allowing her eyes to settle right on the swimming pool. She felt the pool's soothing water easing and even erasing her anxiety, empirically.

In a very stone-colored and khaki pants set, he stepped right onto the terrace. Saul's eyes were just bulging, which caused some wrinkles to appear right across his already wrinkly forehead. "Why you're dressed in that get-up of a swim-suit?" he questioned his wife, Mable. Saul did so, right, before he strutted toward her in a pair of stone-colored loafers.

"Good morning to you, too," spoke Mable, in a starkly dry voice.

Saul took a seat at the table where his wife sat. "You need not bother working out…. Because, in a few days you'll be given a younger—new face, and a slimmer—new body," he told Mable, grinning, if not smirking, artfully.

Voicelessly, she just looked down at Saul.

He just placed the bouquet of *Harlequin Lupines*—right, back, in the center of the table. Saul then gazed, glowingly, at the poisonous flowers with sparkly eyes—glowing, so.

"Why do you so like—'or, so love' those 'fantastically fatal' flowers so 'damn' much? And, when did you become so 'goddamn' vain?"

No longer full of fulsome—or, glowing, for his mouth fell agape, and then Saul's eyes squinted. "Vain? What do you mean?" he cross-questioned.

Mable's glare just penetrated his superficial, ulterior, and exterior— and even interior being. She saw, heard, and smelt things that're down-right detestable…. So, Mable just continued looking way down at Saul; who, once upon a time, had been the only great love of her love-life, or soul-mate, quite supposedly. But, over time, he'd changed…. Neither did she care for Saul's mistaken metamorphosis. He was proving to be a weak and a foolish man, or use-less, and utterly. Mable didn't want or need such male. She thought about her husband's damnably dark debauchery—or damn decadence. Then, Mable just rose from her chair or the table.

"Where you're going?" asked Saul, dumb-founded.

Mable just kept on walking, away.

That particular day, she neither needed nor wanted to touch nor taste any part of the dark debauchee's debauchery, or his decadence. So much had dissipated, already, right, into a state of darkly damnable dissipation. Mable's productively private investigator had solidified such, since.

…He only eyed the woman, who, as of late, had become full-figured, so fairly. Never mind, that her once wrinkle-free and alabaster-like skin was flawless; whose tone and texture both now showed signs of real aging; whose age was now the *new* middle-age—55; whose years managed, un-avoidably, to fade Mable's once beautifully dark-auburn-colored hair, grey, yet partially; whose colorful color complemented, and, rather, surprisingly, her sun-free, if not, un-colorfully controlled complexion; whose coloration still sat very well amid carefully contour eye-brows; whose olive-colored eyes, and perfectly pointed nose, and even glisteningly luscious lips; all of which, just the same, didn't have to maim Mable's sense of self-pride, or her spiritual physicality. It was very good or great, even. That, Saul didn't reach right out to touch his wife or Mable…. Utterly un-emotional, and, mentally aloof, or even, distant, Mable just kept on walking, right, away. He, on the other hand, disappeared from the terrace, confounded, almost, certainly.

She just stood on the pool deck, examining the ultra-marine-colored or sapphire-colored water. Mable inched toward it, pool. Then, she recoiled, so roundly, feeling in-apt, or feeling some measure of in-aptness. Mable then inched even closer to the pool, so allowing her in-appropriate fear to subside, somewhat. The super striking image appeared most in-appropriately, floating in the pool's water…. Its lavender, yellow, plus rose-colored pedals flapped softly yet ominously atop the pool's water.

Mable flinched, so feeling the pretty poisonous pounding in her chest. She wanted and needed to conquer the dangerously dark demon. That had so manifested, it-self, since; and, in the form of a fantastically floral flower—or, a wild flower, just, floating in her pool. Mable took off her swimming robe and then threw it on a deck chair. Next, she took her swimming goggles from around her neck. Fear just wasn't about to stand in her way, any more, today. Mable now moved much closer to the pool.

The pool's water vacillated, causing waves to rise and fall at timely or perfect intervals. The very warm sunlight shone sensationally upon the pool's water, reflecting her image. Mable was pleased, to some extent, as well, by what she saw: a some-what shapely figure. She took one big step and ending up at the edge of the pool alongside the pool's deep end. Inch by inch, Mable just put her right foot forward—or, right, into the pool.

She then signed in roundly rapturous relief, or surprise, actually. As if on cue, Mable transformed herself, right, to a time and place or space, where she wanted or needed to be, again: feeling, fine, and fit, fabulously. She just dove into the pool's very inviting water. The soothing feel of the pool's water just penetrated her tension, further, which had begun to subside or dissipate, anyhow. Mable then waded in the water just long enough to put on her eye wear, or swimming goggles.

After that, Mable kicked once—full-force, forcing herself downward or, under the water. About a minute later, she floated to the top of the water, pool. Pushing off the side of the pool's wall, Mable started to swim. She also intended to swim laps or work out for an hour or so: swimming, and suitably, or perfectly, all of the strokes; which served to set right off, or complement, so circularly, one's physical form: butterfly stroke; breast stroke; front stroke; back stroke; side stroke, and the like.

Mable just swam up and down the stretched out swimming pool of a heavenly and healthy haven…. She allowed the labor of love to just transport her; to a time and a place—or, a space—right, where she so wanted—if not, needed to be, again: on a healthy health-kick. In fact, after Mable finished her laps, she pumped some iron or lifted some weights. Mable then indulged both the sauna and the whirlpool, or the Jacuzzi. Afterwards, *Cianna* delighted her with a mouth-wateringly tasteful brunch of a lunch right on the terrace.

The twenty-something, or young woman steered the fancy motor-car along the very well-paved road that led to the mansion. She just looked at the estate with sad eyes. Eva then shook her head from side to side, frowning, so un-happily, or apparently.... Theirs was no ordinary relationship, mother, and daughter. ...Mable and Eva's extraordinary bond consisted of un-conditional love, mutual respect, and genuine friendship. Thus, whatever Mable decided to do, Eva intended to support her right until the bitter-sweet end.... Mable's happiness would be felt, so deeply, by Eva; and, in the case of sadness, that would be felt, so deeply, by Eva, as well.

After having driven into the driveway, she silenced the *Volvo's* silent engine. And, right, after having grabbed her purse from the front passenger's seat, Eva slid out of the very well-appointed automobile.... She then looked from side to side; and, seeing that both her parents' cars were right there, in their respectively outer parking spaces. Not surprising, either, that during the hotter months of the year—summer, mainly, both Saul and Mable parked in the gigantic garages; which were attached to the mansion.

Eva hurried right into the house.

...She was met by the house keeper; who, now, was dusting the living room's furniture.

"Hi *Cianna*," spoke Eva, "and where's my Mom?"

Cianna replied..., "She's on the terrace and how"—*Cianna* stopped, so suddenly, looking at Eva. She was dashing up the stairs, already. Then, the house keeper only shook her head from side to side.

The reasonably young, short, slim, and, red-haired, and even, casually clad—female, just, tip-toed, right, in silence. Eva did so, as she passed by her father's home-office. That was right down the hall from his seemingly rest-less—if not, love-less bed-room. Eva then made her way, just, like a ghost, toward the terrace, through Mable's seemingly love-less, if not rest-less bed-room; which, she shared with her un-lovable, if not, head-less husband; who, almost, always, seemed to be on edge, lately. Eva knew, too, without a doubt, that, eventually, she'd to face Saul, down. Or, she'd to comment, some-what, on his super shaky—if not, super edgy existence so purported by Mable, her mother.

Approaching Mable from the rear, Eva greeted her..., "Hello Mother, and how're you doing?"

A wide smile popped right onto Mable's face before answering, "My Darlin'—fine, and you?"

Eva said, "I'm okay," and kissing her mother's right cheek. After that, Eva sat adjacently to Mable at the center patio table. "It's looking as though someone's had a super scrumptious lunch, or brunch," stated Eva, as a smile now popped right onto her face.

"Yes, *Cianna* fixed some of my favorites—fruit cock-tail, a 24-hour vegetable salad, some cream of vegetable soup, and a red-baked potato, and even a honey-wheat muffin—"

"GREAT...! I'm so glad, Mom, to see that you're now resuming your health-kick, healthily."

Mable's eyes just lit up with such joy as she expressed, joyously, "My morning work-out was just so wonderful! It's been quite a while, feeling the pool's water relaxing my mind, heart, and, body, and even, spirit—or, entire being, and all, the way it has. And, indulging the sauna—or, the Jacuzzi—OH MY! I feel good all over...!"

Eva commented, "You look good—or, wonderful, too, and, so much younger than your actual age."

...That once joyous twinkle in Mable's eyes—and, that once glorious glow on her face—or, her being, both of which, disappeared, and slowly, but surely. Since, she got right back to her fantastically fateful reality...: her own (real) life. "Darlin', you're just too 'damn' kind...," Mable told her daughter with a trace of sweet rancor or, a bit of bitterness.... Now wasn't the time for any sourness or was it?

Eva locked eyes with Mable and then spoke, "You've always instilled in me the very value of a positive attitude..., a proper diet, and some proper exercise, and even some proper rest, and so forth. Why did you just cast aside your *own* great advice, Mother?" inquired Eva, impatiently, with inquiringly big eyes that're brownish-green, and, captivatingly; "Was it because of some in-discretion of Saul's?" Eva pried, just, a little bit.

"Oh, Eva...!" Mable just griped; "If only, it were that simple.... It's some-times hard trying to keep a positive attitude and all. Your father—well, his lack of discretion—or, true caution, is something that I don't care to talk about—just, yet."

"Why not just go right back to work...? Or, why not just re-assume, or resume your position at the investment company—your company, or you-all's—or, even, yours and Saul's...?"

Absolutely, she looked askance at her daughter with eyes that bulged. "What kind of position...?" Mable cross-questioned Eva's interestingly un-expected question of a suggestion.

"I don't know—well, you surely could be vice-president..., again, or something of the sort."

Dryly, and, staunchly, Mable just informed Eva, "I've no 'goddamn' desire to work amid those sometimes dark, devious, and pitiless—'or, darkly purple-colored' parasites of high finance."

Eva inquired, and, half-heartedly, "Mom, do you still intend to have the plastic—or, the cosmetic surgery?"

With creased brows, a fantastic frown stretched right across Mable's no longer youthful face.

"I always wish you well, Mother. Plus, if ever there's anything that I can do for you or even not do for you—then, pretty please, just say so."

Eva stood up.

"Thank-you…, Darlin'," Mable reciprocated, or responded, so coolly. For, her composure meant something, almost, always.

"…I suppose that I'll see you later…?" Eva ended the supportive yet short but focused and useful visit. After a big good-bye kiss on Mable's left cheek; plus, a very warm hug around her would-be, tight torso; once more, in silence, Eva disappeared—and, was disappointed, some, seemingly.

Mable just looked at the tennis court and then the jogging track. She just had to sulk and then smirk, within. She did so, too, for several days….

Having since exited the high way, Eva now drove the motor car along the roadway that led right to their destination. She just glanced at her mother; who appeared to have been miles away in an utterly un-known place; whose space was most likely suffocative…, some. Looking blankly out the right and front passenger's window, Mable saw nothing but darkness…. Even, though, the great big purplish-orange-colored fire-ball was settled so well in the small and purplish-blue-colored sky. "I hope that everything will turn out well for you, Mother," offered Eva, and concernedly. Was Mable still swallowed up, right, by the bluish-purple-colored sky that was shrinking, superficially?

The medium-sized hospital was in sight, now.

Eva headed right to its parking lot. After having driven into a parking space, she quieted the engine of the car, *Volvo*.

Right, before Saul exited the motor vehicle, he grabbed Mable's small suitcase from the back seat whence he'd sat too quietly…. Perhaps, Saul had been swallowed up, right, by his very own purplish-blue-colored thoughts of a superficially shrinkable sky.

Now, Mable exited the automobile—but only, after having hesitated, interestingly. Naturally, Eva followed Mable's move—or cue, exiting the car right with her mother.

The threesome, or Mable, Eva, and Saul all proceeded to the entrance of the building or, the hospital.

Dr. *Luhuis*, or the plastic if not cosmetic surgeon had told Mable that once she arrived at the hospital…, to go straight up, to the fifth floor. There, preparation for surgery awaited her, without fail.

…On the fifth floor of the hospital, a dark, dumpy, and dutiful nurse received Mable, right away: "How may I help you, Madam?"

She spluttered, some, "Yes, haw—I'm Mrs. Maddox, Mable. Hum—and, I'm here to see—or, I've appointment with Dr. *Luhuis* for surgery."

The nurse commented…, "Very well, then follow me…, please," and leading the way.

Turning around, the nurse informed both Eva and Saul…: "Oh, I'm so sorry but you-all will've to wait in the waiting lounge…, which is right down the hall, and, to the left," and then twirling once again on her heels.

My goodness! These people sure moved fast; or, Mable just thought to herself…. She'd been whisked right away…, and was now lying in some surgical bed. It was almost time for Mable to receive, and roundly, her once young beauty. But, not, before she drifted off….

The bed started to move just too damn fast…. Mable opened her eyes widely. Glaring at the nurse that was pushing the surgical bed—or, pushing her, Mable demanded, "STOP!" She then sat up right, pronto, or PRESTO!

The woman of a nurse was stunned, "excuse me?"

"I said stop…!" demanded Mable, again.

The nurse just looked at her and then spluttered…, "Ma'am—what—where—"

Already, Mable was leaping from the bed, "The soon-to-be surgery is hereby cancelled—'or, it's OFF'—for good!" she proclaimed, and recoiled, so roundly, with a super steely backbone. Had Mable's spinal column turned to beautifully bright steel—just, in a nick of time…?

So very dumb founded…, "Madam, what's the problem? And, where you're going…?" questioned the nurse.

Mable just kept on walking—right, down a passageway. Then, for an un-known reason she just looked sideward. Mable was seeing a very pretty pastel-colored painting of the beautiful but sinister yet informative, and, still, so utterly un-inviting wild-flower: *Harlequin Lupine*. It just hung on the wall. Mable stopped..., so suddenly; for, her eyes now bulged; for, her mouth now agape.... A set of circularly creased wrinkles now appeared right on Mable's forehead. Was she just about to seize or snatch the poisonously pretty picture or painting from the wall; then, slam it right down on the super shiny floor, or deck? Instead, Mable only peered piercingly at the painting or picture.... Was she thinking about touching it...? Mable flinched..., experiencing yet another moment of revelation, on the surface.

She spun on her heels—or utterly un-hospitable slippers, disappearing right on down the extended passageway.... Her steps were light and quick yet quite deliberate....

She'd changed back into her civilian attire.

Saul and Eva both just watched as Mable entered the waiting room of a luxurious lounge.

"Mother, what's happened...?" asked Eva. Right, as a set of circularly creased wrinkles appeared on her own forehead above very bulgy eyes and a wide-open mouth. Eva was astounded or bowled over, apparently, and, very.

"Let's get the hell out of here! NOW...!" Mable ordered.

Standing from a chair, Eva spoke—questioned, and was baffled if not mystified, on the face of it, "What? Fine, but I just don't understand...."

Rising whence he sat comfortably, on a circularly comfortable couch, Saul only looked, and, speechlessly, at his wife. Next, he just trailed behind Mable and then Eva—or, their most devotedly dutiful daughter.

In another passageway—or, hallway..., Mable turned to her daughter and retorted: "JUST, look at me...! Am I really in need of some god-damned face-lift, and all? HUH?"

Eva was dazzled—or speechless, essentially.

"I would've been an unreservedly utter idiot to go against everything that I believe in! Having attempted to beautify, or rather, to pacify my self in such way.... Why, for I'll tell you why. It's because your 'darkly debauched and' so very vain-glorious bastard of a father has since fallen for some 'more beautiful and' *younger* woman—'or, maybe even some *younger* women.'"

Executing an about-face, or facing down Saul—Mable gnarled: "And, I needn't stoop to your damned low level, EVER…!" She continued with real rancor spewing right from her dry mouth, so rancorously, and roundly, if not damnably:

> More, I'm divorcing you because of your adultery! Plus, please, rest assured that I've proof…! Furthermore, your damned existence is so synonymous with those damn wild flowers. That you love only too goddamn well—*Harlequin Lupines.* For you're just as poisonous as they are! You're without a doubt worth-less to me. Being such, I want your weak, foolish, and vain, or adulterous ass out of my house; and, off of my property; or, even, way out of my life by sunset—TODAY, UNDERSTOOD?

Gathering a super second wind, or taking a darkly deep breath for the very dark spat, Mable informed Saul—or spate, if not snarled: "I'm not done with you—JUST, YET!"

He'd started to walk away: or, the new middle-aged; and nondescript; yet, memorable; but, repellent; if not, repulsive; or, repugnant; or even, pretty poisonous, goddamned male peon of a philanderer. So, Saul stopped and then looked back, then listened to Mable that glared at, and even spattered on him: "You, MISTER, may very well think that being 55 years old is the new 45—YET, you're dead wrong, Mister Adulterer! You're going to end up a starkly or a nakedly and a damnably old man—ALONE…!" Next, she whacked him right dead on the face. WHACK! Such slap or smack failed to provoke Saul or even evoke a single expression—or, emotion, quite interestingly.

Mable delivered her final blows, which were both high and low, right, to her soon-to-be ex-husband; who, she looked down—on, rancorously, and roundly, without doubt, or fail.

…With his head hanging low, and his torso hanging even lower, Saul just looked up, in a super subdued manner, at Mable, wordlessly. No words flowed or spewed from his mouth. Most, presumably, he neither wanted nor felt the need to question, or even challenge his soon-to-be ex-wife's absolute accusation of an indictment. He dared not to do it…! Saul, almost, certainly, wished, instead, that Mable just understood the woefully or the wildly wicked world; in which one lived, that so propelled one to transgress, tantalizingly.

Having been put down—or, pushed down, utterly, and, un-mercifully, right, by Mable—or, a super strong slapper, Saul only moseyed away; right, to the receptionist's desk where upon he just telephoned some taxi service or another service of sort, so assumably, or, rather presumably.

Eva just hugged her mother and then confessed, most candidly, "I'm sure glad—that, this terribly tantalizing tribulation is over...!"

Mable and her dutifully devoted, or dedicated daughter, or even only child just left the hospital, together, without Saul, quite, obviously. They're grateful, and, most seemingly, for having risen rightly to the overly onerous occasion. Saul, in all probability, on such occasion, planned to do what else, exactly. Unsurprisingly, their steps were much lighter.... Life was even much brighter for the twosome, or Mable and Eva. They stepped lightly and swiftly yet decisively—on, out the front door of the hospital...; right, on a circularly cool, calm, and candied—or, a very well collected and late afternoon in early fall of 1989.

Much, later, the mirror spoke the utterly unadulterated truth.

Inside her bedroom, Mable looked deeply and proudly at the looking glass, or mirror. She really relished what she saw...: a much stronger woman; who'd been feeble, and, fantastically, in her beliefs. "Nevermore...!" Mable enunciated, or swore, so steadfastly. She then massaged her face, steadily, or slowly: Her soft hands just caressed up and down and all around it—her face, little by little. Mable was ever so careful, too, having been so mindful of the super sensitive areas on her face that showed sure signs of stress or age.... At the end of the day, Mable completed the roundly righteous ritual.

Afterwards, she rose from the dressing table's chair and then turned right out its beautifully bright light. Mable felt good or great if not fabulous, all over—in fact. Mable was certainly confident.... That she *alone* just had to regenerate, and roundly, her own brand new youth-ful-ness, without doubt— or, fail. ...Mable just had to adhere to her strict beliefs of maintaining a very positive attitude; exercising regularly; and, eating properly; and, even, resting adequately, among other things.

"Yes, indeed, I'm already *growing young*...!" Mable so exclaimed, or rather, so proclaimed, right, before she retired to bed, and comfortably, alone. There, Mable dreamt a roundly romantic dream, most, entertainingly. It was all about one of the English Romantic Poet's—or, Percy Bysshe Shelley's (1792-1822) poem...: "Love's Philosophy"; whose very perceptible, or pretty philosophical principles rested quite positively on lust-less love....

Part III

Expectation

Has real expectancy been lost forever?

It was a sultry night in the late spring of 1999.

...Had the young woman prepared for tonight that was known around town as, "Ladies' Night?" Or, had she waited far long enough for such night to come: some super secret rendezvous?

Already attired assiduously..., Kate Kowen floated feverishly into her bedroom. Was some super-normal force compelling her? In any case, it was now time for the total transformation to take place.

Kate opened a drawer of her dresser; and, then, she took out a bright-auburn-colored wig, (so, un-like her naturally brownish-black-colored hair); then, she became someone else: or, a made-up somebody else.... Fortunately, the wig's color just complemented Kate's ebony-colored and good-looking skin; whose covering, or mildly made-up face didn't necessarily up-stage her naturally attractive features: or, very well-arched brows; hazel-colored eyes; sharp nose; chock-full lips, (glitteringly just like 24-carat-gold).

Now, she was peering piercingly at the dresser's mirror, and, almost, smirkily. Was Kate flavoring or just savoring what she saw: a very different-looking female than before?

She blurted out, "I'd better hurry up...!"

Kate then twirled on a pair of high velvety heels. They're pitch-black shoes that complemented, circularly, her jet-black stockings: or, shapely legs, and pitch-black, velvety—form-fitting dress; whose jet-black satiny belt was choking Kate's small waist, most, comfortably. Just, under her breath, some very whispery words sounded out...: "Yes, indeed, it's now-or-nev'r and do-or-die."

...In no time, at all, Kate was right out the front door of her circularly commodious condominium, condo; whose circularly capacious space housed some utterly up-to-date furnishings or, furniture...: leather furniture, marble tables, European tapestries, porcelain, crystal, and so forth.

In a some-what wrinkly and dark denim—pants suit, the young, tall, and Mulatto-looking man accelerated right into the little dinette of a kitchen.

He then snatched open the leaky icebox. Suede Stuart was after a very cool bottle of Vodka.... Did he really have time for a quick small drink...? After having grabbed a spotty glass from a circularly crumbly cabinet, Suede poured him-self a nice-sized drink. After that, Suede flavored a long swallow of it—poison.

Next, Suede left the kitchen carrying the poisonous drink.

Why wasn't he on the move, way? After all, it was "Ladies' Night."

Suede savored another long swallow of the poison on his way to his bedroom.

There, in the bed room, Suede pranced to a circularly cracked mirror on the wall and then looked aslant at his reflection. He looked like a down-rightly decadent man. Has it been so hard for Suede to down-play his life or even past life? "Oh hell…! I look all right," professed Suede, "considerin' all that I've been through—a goddamn'd grinder."

He reached, rapidly, for an old-looking hat that sat on an old, messy, and crumbly dresser. It ended up right on Suede's un-shaven, and blackish-brown-colored head of hair. His poisonous drink even ended up, right, on the dresser; but, only, after Suede downed the very last of the poison, or Vodka.

After that, he pivoted on some roundly run-down heels and then left the bed-room.

Once inside of the living room, Suede grabbed a set of keys from the worn-down coffee table. He then patted the left back pocket of his pants. It appeared that something or another was bulging right through the blackishly blue-colored denim.

Next, Suede zipped right out the front door of his utterly un-tidy flat of an apartment: A flat that probably should've been flattened…, already. Or, it just needed to be torn down; to be re-built, and re-decorated, and even re-marketed….

Now, outside, in an almost empty parking lot of the rental apartment building—or, complex, Suede slid right into his rustily red Regal…. He then fired up the car's engine. A smoke was subsequently in order. So, Suede fired it up, too: a Marlboro Light; which was taken from its pack in the car's glove compartment. Before inhaling a long draw of the poison…, he turned on the car's cassette player; where upon the sounds of Kool and the Gang's old but top, or musically big hit—"Ladies Night" sounded out…, rightly. Suede sung along, so rightly, with the super soulful Rhythm and Blues' band. He did so, while making his way right into the sultrily and bluely black-colored night…, puffing, poisonously, to boot.

Right, on the Tarot Cards, was it a sultry or a sinister or even a sweet Ladies' Night…?

Club Candy was the place to be or, so it seemed.

The very pretty psychedolic night-club stood statuesquely, somewhat, along U.S. 1, in Hallandale, Florida, standing, there, in all its roundly retroactive rareness. The movingly fast sounds of the Isley Brothers' "That Lady," played on the club's stereo; whose sporadically spacious, high, and wide, and even loud speakers blasted out. Psychedelic lights just lit up the semi-smoky, semi-sized, and semi-full room…; whose occupants just sat about, drinking, smoking, chatting, grinning, smooching, butt watching, and the like.

Garbed, right, in a slinkily off-white mini-dress, the thirty-something, and whitish-tan-colored woman sashayed; right, to the long, broad, and open bar, in a pair of very off-white-colored shoes; whose high heels were fraying, outwardly; yet, she swayed on, with her head up, busty chest out, and belly way in, and, even, seemingly, quite forcefully.

Kitten approached it, or the drinking counter. "Howdy," she greeted the reddish-looking, middle-aged, and able-bodied man, or bartender; "and, I'll have my usual poison."

"Hey Kit," purred Dex, smilingly—"it's comin' right up…," doing an about-face.

He was dressed in a dark, wrinkly, and cottony shirt and pants; or, the short, stout, and darkish-tan-colored man, who staggered right to the bar.

Trembling, some, "Wut's kookin'—or, bakin'…, Bab," whispered the man; "yoo prite litle kooke? The nam's Big Slim an yoors, fer rel?"

After a very quick exam, Kitten just dismissed the man: "Really, you don't want to know…," and then sipping some of her drink; which, Dex had since delivered; after which, he'd just serviced another customer of a drinker, and, promptly.

"…Don't over-luk me…, jest, yet. Koz, hoo nos, I ma jest be wut yer lookin' for—"

"You like inflatin' yourself?"

"I'd lik too—"

Frowning, or scowling, "PLEASE," Kitten spoke, rather gloweringly, in a circularly cynical but very clear yet cold and authoritative if not superior voice or tone; "JUST, leave me be—since, something's roastin'!"

The man was just about to sit down—next, to Kitten—then, perhaps, he thought better of it—stumbling, sideward, instead. "O?" he just slurred, "I prizoom that yer wurkin' an ol," trembling, some, still.

…Kitten only glared at Big Slim with roundly red-hot fire right in her reddish-colored eyes.

"Ha! I got 30 dolers—"

"That won't ev'n buy you a damn peep or peek! Now go on and scat or, GET…!"

He just grabbed Kit's arm, which only a minute or two ago, was well occupied with her poisonous drink. It now sat right in front of her on the bar counter, poisonously.

"Get your goddamn cotton-pickin' hands off of me," Kitten grimaced and then shrieked or snapped, coldly; "you, goddamn'd VIPER!"

"…FIN…! An, it's yoor big los…, Luv." Big Slim shrunk back with wrinkly brows, pouty lips, bent shoulders—and, was snubbed, or slighted, if not insulted, to a great extent.

He stumbled away. She breathed a sign of relief, superficially.

…Kitten even veered her position on the wooden bar-stool that was snapping right apart or dry-rotting. She did such—right, before gulping down some of that pretty poisonous drink of hers, most poisonously.

Kate swept into Club Candy.

A man that sat near the hot spot's entrance greeted her as she passed right by his table: "Hallo Ms. Lady."

Except, for a slight nod of her head and a slight smile…; Kate ignored the darkly gangster-like male so garbed in starkly dark grey. She instead went straight to the drinking counter.

Arriving at it—bar, Kate just questioned Kitten, "Is this seat taken?" referring to a vacant seat that was next to Kitten.

"Hi, and go on, sit."

"Good! And, thanks."

Right away, Kitten commented and then inquired, "I haven't seen you before. You're new in town?"

Sitting very comfortably right on the crumbly bar stool, Kate replied, in brief, "New—hardly," putting her small, black, and velvety purse down on the counter, aside.

"Oh?" muttered Kitten, looking at Kate, and, quite, inquiringly; "I'm sure that I haven't seen you before—"

She cut in, coolly, "And, vice-versa."

Rather, beamingly, the bartender, or Dex approached Kate…, "Hi and what's your drinking pleasure?" he asked.

"Hum, some Scotch, and a glass of cool water to chase it, please."

He acknowledged her request, "It's comin' right up," and then went to fetch Kate's drink—or poison.

She wasn't finished with the inquiry, just, yet…: "You're waitin' for somebody?"

Kate just looked around the night club and volunteered nothing.

"Well, if you're not meetin' anybody, or somebody—then, maybe, we could or should just keep each other company…. Or, just, enjoy one another. By the way, what's your name?"

Kate only looked at Kitten and again volunteered nothing.

"Hey, I'm just tryin' to be nice—"

"My name's Jade," lied Kate.

"And mine's Kit—or, Kitten."

Dex, or the bartender intervened, "Here you are, Ms. Lady," placing Kate's—or, Jade's drink down—right, in front of her on the drinking counter.

"Put it right on my tab, Dex," Kit insisted right before she flavored or savored some more of her drink, or poison.

"…That's okay—but, thanks…," expressed Jade, and reaching right for her purse to pay for her own damned poisonous drink; "I've it—"

"I insist! Dex…," Kitten persisted, adamantly, or inflexibly.

She just gave in, reluctantly, "All right then…, and thanks," said Jade with a roundly reluctant smile, which turned suspicious, on the face of it.

The bartender complied…, finally, and then spun on his heels. Or, he disappeared to service some other customer or another customer.

Was she now slipping into some utterly un-customary role? Kate—or Jade—as it were, settled right down onto the bar stool. Next, Jade, if not Kate flavored or savored a very lengthy swallow of her drink before she spoke or enquired: "So, what's goin' on with you, Kitten?"

"Haw—nothin', well—actually, if you want to know the stark-naked truth, I'm out to get you—

"Say what?"

"Normally, I don't make passes at women, but—"

"Sorry, Kit," Jade just apologized, "but, I'm 100% straight," and then gulping down some of her drink—or Scotch—or even poison.

Jade then finished her drink and its chaser…; grabbed her purse from the bar counter; stood up from the bar stool…; told Kitten good-by; and, was about to disappear, elsewhere; but, not, before Kitten responded, rapidly, and roundly: "Listen Jade, please don't just think that I'm always AC 'cause I'm not. I'm also DC or I can be DC/AC, both. I just had this wonderfully wild fantasy…, you know. And, haw—I couldn't or wouldn't just dis-credit you, lookin' all fancy and sexy and all—"

"No biggie. And, again, no thanks…."

"Why not re-consider…? 'Cause we can have ourselves a real Ladies' Night—"

"…I don't think so—but, you go 'head and have a good—or, a great night."

"Uh-huh, and ain't nothin' happenin', but you gettin' right with one of these hard-bitten and low-bred dudes that're staggerin' or struttin' 'round."

Jade scanned the room and then spoke, honestly, or, most seemingly: "As a matter of fact, Kitten, you're right," and seeing, curiously, a ruggedly Mulatto-looking male strutting to another end of the elongated bar.

Both Kate and Kitten were done….

He took a seat at the drinking counter.

"Hi Pretty Lady," voiced the metallic voice.

Kate—or, better yet, Jade replied, "Hi," and then took a seat next to Suede.

"I just can't help sayin' that you're lookin' mighty fine…, Ms. Lady!" commented Suede, emphatically.

"Thanks."

Raising his hand up in the air, Suede seized the bartender's attention.

"Hey Man and long time no see…," said Dex, as he approached both Suede and Jade; "What's been happenin'…?" he queried, grinningly.

Suede answered, "Ahhh—I've been away, on business."

With furrowed brows, or suspicious eyes, and his grin having since turned right into an affectedly warp-sided smile, Dex asked, "Oh yeah?"

"Yeap…! Now, please, just, let me have a drink—some Vodka, for me. And, for the lady…," looking now, at Jade; "what'll it be?" questioning her, rather smilingly.

With un-furrowed brows, yet curious eyes, and her grin having since turned right into an un-affected smile; Jade answered, at first thought, most, probably: "Some more Scotch—and, please, another very cool glass of water to chase it."

Dex responded, "Okey-dokey," and then spun away.

How was this day or night ending…? And, who, if anyone intended to win…?

Drinking her poison and puffing right on a poisonous cigarette, quite poisonously; Kitten just glared at Jade and Suede—both, right, from the other end of the long bar. Without haste, Jade sat right—next, to him, Suede. Then, he ingratiated her, Jade, obviously, or most presumably, with what, though?

More than likely, Kitten knew such answer…, or she knew the likes of him, Suede.

And, who so ever was right next to Kitten, so conceivably, heard her murmuring meanly—way, under her breath…: "Yeah, I know his damn kind only too goddamn well…. Suede's nothin' but a damn'd love-lorn—and, a damn'd hard-boil'd—or, a goddamn'd felon…!" She signed, externally, and then puffed on, as well as drunk on, poisonously.

…Kitten just looked away from the two—Jade, and Suede—and then finished her drink, then her cigarette. Had the twosome's circularly colorful chattiness begun to aggravate her, if not alienate her, Kitten? If so, she was going to do something about it, apparently. Kitten just veered her position on the bar stool to check out the scene, better, and, much.

Her presumable peers paced and danced all about…, while Fleetwood Mac's big top hit—"Little Lies," just, blared out. The down-beat if not up-beat sounds sent a colorfully cheery chill, quite possibly, all through Kitten's overly shapely body. It did so, in anticipation of a very possible get-together.

Since, a very superficially eye-catching or even attention-grabbing yet super shadowy-looking and very well-built male danced toward her in a pair of semi-shiny shoes. …In a very in-formal way…, he was clothed right in an off-colored khaki—pants set, dancing, sinfully, onward.

He spoke, "Howdy."

"Hi Sweetie," purred Kitten.

"What's cookin'?"

"Me. And, if it's to your likin', you, or us."

"I do like what I'm hearin'!"

Kitten tossed her head of fake and reddish-blond curls that went badly with her wrinkly and whitely tan-colored features; whose appearances were all made up. Ultimately, she responded, "Those close to me, call me, Kit, or Sweet Pea."

"Is that so?" asked the male, and inching much closer to her, Kitten, or Kit, or even Sweet Pea.

"Sure 'nough."

"I'd like to get really close to you—"

The seductress only smiled, seductively, or most seemingly.

"Is it gonna cost me…? 'Cause I'm a little short on cash but long on love-makin'. And, I'll truly set you on fire…!" so volunteered the male with a super seductive smile or smirk (of his very own…); whose teeth appeared to have been both cleaned and polished, somewhat.

Sweet Pea, Kit, or Kitten looked deliberately up and down and even all around the male's marvelously muscled body. She then asked him, "You wantta get the hell outta here...?" Was she cutting the male some slack; or, was she giving him a break—even, though, he couldn't rightly afford a night of tantalizingly toasty thrills, or circularly cheap thrills, more than likely?

He expressed, pleasingly, or better yet, rather beamingly, "Yeah, let's go..., Sweet Thang!" and stepping aside, some; but, not, before he caressed Sweet Pea's or Kitten's big butt, which was protruding, un-prettily.

"How right you are..., Sweetie," Kit—or, Sweet Pea purred, standing right up.

Kitten—or, Kit then looked unkindly at Jade before she snatched her pocketbook from the counter. After that, she just wriggled away, un-steadily, and then steadily...: And, what about that poisonously alcoholic tab or bill of hers...?

Jade only watched, as Kitten and her date both disappeared right from sight....

On the other hand, Suede watched her—or Jade, kindly. Did he really like her kind...? Before taking a very long swallow of Vodka—or, poison, he admitted to her: "I like you."

"I like you, too," Jade reciprocated.

"You don't think that I'm just a washy wind-bag do you?"

She cross-questioned, "What do you mean?"

"Well, 'cause I've been ramblin' on 'bout nothin'...."

At first, Jade chuckled lightly. Then, she told him, "I'm enjoyin' your company."

Not exactly out of the dark gray-blue, he grabbed hold of Jade's left hand. "I'd really like to enjoy you, more," Suede spoke, softly, or sensuously, or even sensually, if not sexually, largely.

"Oh?"

"Yeah—it's so true...!"

It seemed that she was waiting both anxiously and eagerly, right, for the proposition, which came in no time, at all: "I really do want you—" cried Suede, continuing....

"Yeah...?"

He caressed and then rubbed Jade's leg, then offered her a colorfully, if not a circularly cozy compliment...: "...You feel just as good as you look, Luv."

Speechless, or bowled over, she just stared at Suede.

...The soulfully smooth sounds of Kool and the Gang's old yet top hit "Too Hot" just sounded out...; psychedelic lights lit the room up; and, some sinfully sensual or sensuous scent or even smell suffused the air round about; plus, the two appeared both willing and ready to just get about the evening— or, night, seemingly, without any fright.

Suede suggested, "Why don't we go somewher', else?"

Jade asked, "Such as?" So, Jade wasn't about to give him the heave- ho. Oh no! Was it now time to get going? Or, no more going slow...?

"We should just go wherev'r we can to get loose and then close."

"Yeah, I suppose that we've dilly-dallied, long, enough," commented Jade, and finishing her drink.

Suede agreed so very easily, "Sure, you're right...," and finishing his drink, now.

Jade then inquired, "By the way, how're you travelin'?"

"I've a ride—"

"Whoa!" she interjected, concernedly, and very; "I may be out for an outwardly wreck-less night of fun. But, I aim to be alive, tomorrow...! Listen here, you really ought not to drive or me—"

"What're you sayin'?"

"You're more than just a wee-bit tipsy and—"

"O.K.," he yielded; "we can just fetch a taxi...."

Jade remarked, "Sounds good or damn good.... And, we both can just collect our rides—or, our cars..., later."

"Hey Dex...!" Suede called after the industrious bar keeper that was moving all around, quite industriously.

Servicing some other couple or another couple..., Dex answered right back, "Yeah!"

"Call me a taxi—Bro!"

Shaking his head, Dex obeyed—or, he made the call.

Standing up, "And, we should be on our merry way," Suede told Jade, "since we don't wantta miss our ride and all."

Standing up, as well, she concurred, "for sure."

At first, Suede stumbled, some, and then gathered his composure as he stepped away; but, not, before he left what looked like a very wrinkly ten- dollar-bill on the bar counter. "This way, Luv—just follow me," spoke Suede to Jade.

Jade garnered her purse from the counter. Next, she looked down at the two poisonously empty glasses that so sat on it, drinking counter. Suede's and hers, or their poisonous drinks were finished. And, apparently, something else was just about to start. Or, had something already started…? Jade spun on her heels and then disappeared right behind Suede.

Suede glanced over his shoulder, apparently, to ensure that Jade was indeed in tow, or, en route.

"Wait up! The taxi isn't goin' to leave us…," said Jade, stepping on, a little un-steady, or un-steadily.

He conceded, "You're so right, Luv," yet zoomed right out the club— or, the door of an exit, anyway, and unsteadily.

Outside of Club Candy, both Suede and Jade just waited for the taxi cab and a short wait it was, without a doubt.

"Here it comes!" Suede exclaimed.

The taxi came to super screechy stop right in from of them. Then, the taxi driver asked through the vehicle's semi-open window, "Y'all called for a taxi—"

"Yup…!" Suede replied.

"Well, let's go. Or, MOVE IT…!"

Suede opened up the back door of the cab for Jade; she slid right into it and right before him.

"Where to?" questioned the driver with an easterly European accent.

Suede murmured, "Hum—"

"WELL?"

"Motel Moony," Jade responded, rapidly.

The taxi driver then acknowledged, "All right," driving off, speedily.

…Suede gave Jade a circularly curious look as he just sat back in his seat: "What do you know 'bout Hotel Honey—or, Motel Moony?" he probed with a small smile that turned quickly into a giant grin.

…She said nothing and only offered him a nakedly naughty smirk.

"What're you really 'bout, Hun? Huh?"

"Ask me no questions—and, I'll tell you no lies."

"Okay, but I've to just say—that, I sure hope that my funds are long enough—"

"Don't worry 'bout it, for everything's been planned, arranged," Jade told Suede, smirkingly.

"Oh?"

Once, again, she said nothing and only offered him a nakedly naughty smirk.

The driver—or, a dull-dressed, light-tannish, and hard-spoken man negotiated the taxi-cab south easterly along U.S. 1, in Hallandale, Florida.

...Kate only stared out the taxi's super spotty window, staring at the starkly dark-naked distance. What was she wondering, possibly, if anything, at all? Why, too, her cloak-and-dagger persona; was it thus necessary that she remained in disguise, or incognito...?

The taxi driver announced, "Well, we're here and that'll be $7.50."

Suede just blurted, "I've it, with some luck...," and taking $8.00 from his very washed-out wallet; "here...," he told the driver and then passed over the very wrinkly money.

"Thanks," said the driver, crankily, "and y'all have a good night."

Unfortunately, and, so utterly, the taxi-driver just presumed and even assumed that Suede's little change was his little tip.

"Hey! Where's my change?" questioned Suede, quite quickly.

He apologized, and, most crabbily, "Oh—sorry...," and then handing back Suede's modest change, or the meager 50 cents.

Jade just stepped from the cab, vehicle.

While looking askance at the driver..., Suede exited the vehicle, also.

The taxi driver then roared off, roaringly, or, right, into a very tight-fistedly thorny and Thursday night: or, Ladies' Night.

Interestingly, that Jade led the way. Both approached the front door of Motel Moony, or a small-sized, dark-colored, plus externally deserted place; which was perched alongside U.S. 1, beneath some over-grown trees; which failed, fantastically, to camouflage the motel's subdued yet colorful enough, neon-sign; whose letter coloring was that of a drearily dark rainbow right on a colorfully bright and moony night. Was Suede and Jade's night turning out all right...?

He opened the door for her and then they both went right in.

Arriving at the receptionist's desk, both Jade and Suede were greeted by an old, white, and nondescript—at best, or worst—maybe, a darkly bright ghost of a woman: "Good evenin'," spoke the woman in a haunting voice.

"Hi, and—haw, we'd like a nice room...," said Suede; "seein' that the place's empty and all."

"Oh?" the woman attested, apathetically, or without any interest; "I'm so sorry, but all of our rooms are booked..., solidly. What's more, looks can be rather deceivin'—to be sure."

"Honey, you've forgotten…," Jade just interpolated; "Ma'am, we've a reservation under the name, Hodge."

The woman retracted, "Oh, very well, then—or, I just need to check or even confirm that."

…The brightly dark woman of a ghost left and then ended up right at a computer terminal of some sort.

…With his brows raised, and his eyes pierced right on her, and even his lips pretty puckered; Suede just eyed Jade for a minute or two, circularly, and most curiously.

The woman then re-appeared as well as confirmed, and circularly, the Hodges' reservation and even speaking…: "All right…, Mr. and Mrs. Hodge it seems that everything's in order."

Per, chance, or, intuitively, Jade was given some paper work of some kind to fill out. Afterwards, she gave the woman some crisply cold cash.

Suede blurted out, "What's it costin' us—Luv?"

"Everything's covered," answered Jade, in a big hurry.

The ghostly woman or receptionist stated, very, suspiciously, "Okay," and looked sideways at the pair, or the twosome…; "here's y'all room key," handing it right over, at a snail's pace, to Suede, first, and then to Jade; who accepted it—key, with a sideward smile; which evolved rapidly, and roundly, into an in-direct frown, on the surface.

Was there some cause for some disgrace or some dishonor?

Right, away, Suede just accepted the key—or, it, from Jade and then responded with a direct smile that evolved, immediately, into a great big one, smile—or smirk: "Thanks…," he ended the circularly chary if not odd check-in, smilingly, or quite smirkily.

The utterly un-likely pair then spun on their roundly respective heels. Next, they disappeared from the little lobby of a reception area, en route to its little elevator.

After a few minutes or so, the elevator's door opened right up, on the second floor of Motel Moony; whose utterly un-colorful passageway wasn't that wide or high yet negotiable enough. Such enabled both Suede and Jade to pass right through it, so un-encumbered, as well as in darkly stark-naked silence. The hall way needed some more lighting, for sure.

Using a rustily thick key, Suede unlocked the door of room number, TWO, where upon a dim, small, and barely furnished space greeted them. It did such, with the very basic help of some very weak lighting; which shone right through the very ultra-thin drapes of the medium-sized picture window. Obviously, it was the out-side street's lighting—shining right in, through the only un-open-able window in the room.

Moving first into the room..., Jade commented, "Well, I suppose that it'll do—"

"Of course," offered Suede; "it'll have to...," moving into the room, secondly, and shutting the room's door, thirdly.

Next, Jade got comfortable: she put her purse down; her shoes came off; she turned a little lamp atop a little table on and then off, then, on, again.

Curiously, Suede asked Jade, "What's wrong, Luv...?" and then got comfortable, himself. He flopped right down on the lightly made up bed.

"Nothin', well, do we really need the light? Seein' that we've already some street-light—or, moon-light and all?" she cross-questioned.

"Please, Luv, just let the light stay right on. 'Cause, I want to see you and see what I'm doin', fully."

"Fine," remarked Jade, who just left the light, right, alone...; "and, I almost forgot...." She dashed toward her purse that lay on the little dresser of the wide-open bedroom, or studio-like space. Perhaps, it was nothing more or less than a one-room and would-be efficiency; which, she had rented for the eventual evening, or a starkly or even a darkly naked night.... Was it right...? Jade got a very pretty, purplish-black incense of some genus and a short yet broad and blackish-purple candle right from her purse.... She then lit up both with some haste.

"What're you doin'..., Luv?"

"I'm just settin' the scene," suggested Jade; "and, why don't you get more comfy or comfier."

Evidently, he took her suggestion and very well. Since, Suede didn't waste any time getting un-dressed, and comfortably. Did he have a need, too, of a very poisonous crutch to lean on..., for support; while Jade disappeared right with her purse in tow into the bath room—right, after she lit that candle and incense—up? Right after Jade left the room..., Suede fired up a cigarette. It came from his shirt's pocket that hardly bulged, beforehand. On, the other hand, his wallet bulged well beforehand, and, apparently, from the left back pocket of his pants. Subsequently, Suede undressed....

Once more, did Suede necessitate such crutch because of his apparent eagerness, or anxiousness, or what, exactly? He looked tense, some, or over-wrought about something or another...; but, what, exactly...? His elongated puffing, palpably, or obviously, just wasn't enough—not, until Suede began coughing. That was when he surely killed the poison, which was poisoning if not killing him, most, observably. Suede even settled back on the little bed whilst the poisonous after-smoke inescapably swallowed him right up. It did so, right, with the nastily smelly ash-tray, which sat next to the slow-burning incense and candle; all of which now sat on another little table…. Suede shut his eyes and then opened them, bit by bit, while just lying back on the bed.

Now, Jade re-appeared back on the scene all freshened up…, rather, imaginably. That, Jade was a beautifully bright sight right on this dark, late, and progressive night. Neither did she appear to have any fright…. Nor was Jade probably looking to have any type of fight; or, was she…?

"Well," Suede just declared, "it's now time, Luv, for us to make love. And, you're so damn lovely," and then smiling a super strained smile.

Kate, or Jade, as it were, was clad in nothing—but, a big, black, and fluffy-looking towel. She put her purse down on the little settee in the little living room of the little open space. After that, Jade slid right into the little bed, whose occupant only smiled minus any strain, right, now. What did the two now hope to gain rightly if any thing, at all?

Jade reciprocated…, finally, "Thanks, and that it is—time"; since, she got a bit more comfortable with Suede's help, of course: That fluffy-looking, black, and big towel was removed, almost, immediately, from her person by Suede; who was openly naked, now.

"On second thought, Luv, we don't really need the light…," admitted Suede, "'cause we've already some very nice candle-light—" just, throwing the bed cover, back.

"That we do."

He secured that dim lighting of a little lamp and then progressed the night, and, rather improperly, per chance.

After it—night, did Jade intend to get and then remain tight with him, Suede?

Not exactly out of the nakedly dark blue, he whispered right in Jade's ear, "You're just as sweet and lovely, Luv, as that super sweet incense that's burnin' bright enough."

The candle's light illuminated the room, through out; and, the incense permeated a mellifluous scent, all about; and, the sensuous or sensual or even sexual scene has been set. What was he or she to do next…?

At first, Suede just kissed Jade very slowly. Then, his roundly red-hot tongue sped things up, quite considerably, as it seemingly melted right in her mouth; whose lips now glittered just like 18-carat-gold under the gorgeously glittery candle-light's hold.

"That's right…," murmured Suede, in super sheer delight; "so just lie right back and relax, Luv," and feeling Jade stretching out. She even shivered some even though the room was warm, and, comfortably, now.

"Oh!" she mumbled, "it's been so—"

"What?" he interjected.

"LONG!"

"Well, Luv, your wait's now OVER…!" declared Suede…; "for, the time's right, TONIGHT!"

…Had she carried a colorless condom covertly, right, on her person—evidently: "Here," Jade articulated, absolutely; "you'll have to use this," and producing that circularly carnal obstacle of an overly overt obstruction.

"A damn'd rubber"—Suede was cut right off and then cut right down in a great big hurry.

"That's right…!" Jade cut right in, hurriedly.

"AHHH, now come on, Luv," he whined and then thought better of it, clearly—"Screw it…!" Suede submitted, most saltily.

Yet, even so, in no time, at all, he became very productive, sexually, by producing….

Softly, Jade just requested—or, ordered—or, even, demanded: "Slow down."

Suede paid Jade no never mind—or, damn attention, and went about his sexual quest, almost, self-centeredly.

"Wait!" she squalled; "Let's just—"

He squawked, "Ain't no more damn waitin'…, WOMAN!"

The lecher's roundly rough hands moved and poked so lecherously up and down and all around her erogenous zone or zones, as it were.

"OOOH," Jade moaned; "AHHHH!"

"You're ready…, Luv?" queried the leech, or Suede; "Just hold on…," he ordered—right, before the inevitable entry was seized; and, right, before she demanded—or, requested, for him to just slow down, AGAIN.

…Had Suede's blood begun to ferment, feverishly, for he perspired, un-prettily?

Right, now, how did Jade feel, and truly, about Suede's roundly rocky rhythm: just, rocking, and rocking, to and fro—or, back and forth, as though there was no damned tomorrow?

Mute…, she just lay right in a saltily dark ocean of nakedly—if not, blatantly bare barbarism beneath a super strong-willed man…; whose strong-arm conduct, or damnatory strong-hold, was about to cease, quite probably.

Not long after their sexual adventure began…, did it end and much to Suede's great dismay; still, he seemed a tad delighted…: "I've since satisfi'd you..., Luv?" Suede inquired, masculinely, inquiring about his masculinity, or maleness.

Jade squeaked, "Let's just rest for a while—"

"...Rest?" the damner just shrieked, damnably; "Luv, I'm just gettin' start'd..."; or, so he thought....

"Just rest...!" she ordered or commanded Suede.

Jade had felt the absolutely awful muscle of Suede's weight and even seen it in his eyes. What had she gotten herself in to...? Had Jade aimed right for an adventurous night of nakedly, if not roundly raw sex, or boldly black barbarity...? Jade just placated (or pacified) Suede, "Sugar, I've climaxed, a few times, already. Now, I'd really like to"—she stopped, suddenly, and then looked obliquely at Suede. On the face of it, he was asleep and soundly. Jade just mumbled and grumbled or rumbled way under her breath...: "Good, and goddamn you—Suede! You little—black barbaric bastard!" Both listless and breathless, she crawled cautiously from the exceedingly creased bed in a state of starkly or harshly dark damnation, most conceivably.

...So damnified, and crumbling, Jade just stumbled to the chair where her clothes lay. There, she just dressed and then sat down, by chance—and, by design.... Next, in a not so round about way, Kate or Jade, as it were, just looked eagle-eyed or even wild-eyed at Suede and then whined beneath her breath: "Oh, my! How could Suede have been so damned rough—or, tough, forceful? And, I'd bargained for a night of more than just a little run-of-the-mill sex, yet"—signing, regretfully, or rather seemingly.

She just signed in down-right disgust; and, shook her head in down-right dis-belief; and, even, dis-carded the pang in her abdomen, down-rightly, or, quite imaginably; then, Jade just glared at Suede most contemptuously.... She, almost, certainly, held him right in circular contempt, and, circularly; he, who was still sprawled out on the bed; and, most, likely, he felt no pain from his most recent and darkly damnable gain. But, was Suede sane, genuinely? And, what was Jade's aversion toward Suede all about, truly? Likewise, did she now want or need to oust him in a very bad way, right, from her motel room...? Jade enunciated, or spoke, so softly, to be damn sure...; "I can sure use something, a drink—or, a cigarette...," standing up.

She just tiptoed to another nearby chair, where upon Suede's shoddy things lay. Jade was about, too, to take a cigarette right from the pocket of his shirt. She instead grabbed Suede's well worn-out wallet ... without a sound and then opened it. Nothing had prepared Jade and Kate for what their eyes saw—NOTHING, at all! Kate and Jade only stared in starkly dark silence at the nakedly bald-faced photograph of Suede and another man just kissing....

"Oh, no…!" Kate screeched and was so repulsed if not repelled and roundly, rather seemingly.

It seemed that absolute apprehension grabbed hold of Kate, tightly, as she just looked at the back of the little snap shot or, tiny photo. "Oh, no, so he's a closet-queen…," rebuked Kate, and, roundly, with highly raised eyebrows, and lightly, if not brightly brown or hazel-colored—wide-open eyes. What was written on the back of the photograph, more than likely, caused a callously cheerless chill to zip right up and down her spine.

In record-breaking time, Kate read and then re-read the sensationally simple saying: **Hoosegow '97**. Agape, and absolutely, she was apprehended, apparently, by the little yet bright and super stunning or super shocking snap-shot of a picture. Quite simply, Kate saw underneath Suede's damnably dark persona. That surely wasn't the beautifully or the circularly nor the colorfully colorful colors of a rainbow on a beautiful, moony, and pleasant night, right? Stumbling, some, Kate just stammered, "OH, MY GOD! He's gay, no—yes, or bi-sexual—what…? And, I just don't understand…."

So quickly, she took one of Suede's cigarettes; and, lit it with his little lighter; and, then, inhaled the palpably pleasurable poison intently and then froze, fundamentally. Without doubt or fail, Kate wasn't frozen for very long. Because, she put Suede's little photo back, and hastily, inside his wallet—disturbed—or, revolted, at best—or worst, so very disgusted by him—Suede; who, now propelled her to just pace perplexedly about the room, puffing, un-prettily, or most poisonously.

Kate consequently, or better, subsequently, halted, right, in the middle of the room, damned, most damnably. Open-mouthed, she only eyed Suede. Had Kate realized ultimately that her ultimate, sexual adventure—or fantasy, as it were, was over—or, so finished? Or, better yet, was Kate through being bastardized, and badly, or seemingly, by Suede's utterly under-ground guise? Eventually, some words spewed right from Kate's open mouth: "I don't have any more anticipation, or *expectation*, for this Ladies' Night, none, at all. As, a matter of fact, I'm so ending this super spurious she-bang—right, now…!" She did so, also, while flavoring or savoring some more of that poison; plus, again, grimacing, and eyeing Suede, so grotesquely, or quite suspiciously; he, who was obviously still stunning or shocking her, to a large extent.

Wasn't it pathetically paradoxical…? That just several hours earlier, Kate, or rather, Jade and Kitten both might've experienced yet another sexual fantasy—or adventure…? Neither was Kitten under-handed—but, instead, so down right up front…. None the less, that Jade—or, Kate had her very own damned thoughts and damned actions to contend or deal with soon, enough: The circularly climatic consequences of some sexual—if not, some damning exploit of a fantastic fancy; which was played out falsely, or, treacherously.

She just killed that poison of an extinguishable cigarette in that nastily smelly ash tray of Suede's. After that, Kate swayed right into the rest room, restlessly, and, most visibly. She then staggered on, stopping right in front of the sink's little mirror of a looking glass. Kate peered so penetratingly at her reflection in the looking glass of a little mirror. What, precisely, did she see, above all, beneath her cloak-and-dagger persona…? Kate fluffed up and then patted down her wig then fluffed it up, yet again. She possibly wondered, as well, did Suede or the swayer sway more towards the sexually straight or the sexually crooked. If he were out of bed, or up and about, soberly; or, more, to the point, could or would Suede just continue to mask, or even un-mask his real sexuality to Kate or Jade?

Granted, that, they, in all probability, could or would never know the truth concerning Suede's true, sexual character, or his sexual identity. Since, Jade and Kate both very soon disappeared, together. Plus, both were equally and definitely distraught, quite plausibly, about their own fancifully ill-fated, sexual adventure, or venture: or, even, vision, without a trace of ever having been there and done that. Was it just some sort of very bad dream of a nastily naked and a damnably dark nightmare…; which feasibly flustered her—Kate, or even Jade—the two—an utterly un-likely pair of a twosome, or duo? The one having been so roundly real and the other having been fabulously, if not fantastically false or forced…. Had greed or some other poisonous (deadly) sin caused their expectations or anticipations or even the lack thereof?

Part IV

Conclusion

What is in a short story?

It essentially if not typically concerns itself with a single awareness—or, a single point of view (*P.O.V.*), stroke—struggle, and affect—or effect; whose clash, and climax, plus conclusion are almost always compressed and charged: in some way, or another way, or even some other way. Short though it may very well be—still, a short story ought not to lack other fundamentals, or, essentials: setting, story, and, plot, and, even, characterization—and, of course, theme. After all, we just do not want to know about some character's frame of mind or the lack thereof; or, about some character's conduct or the lack thereof. Moreover, why, in effect, some character has been affected in some way, and, not, some other way, or even, another way; or, more, some character, whose life's conflict ought to reach some sort of climax and even close.

Equally important, what is the short story all about? What is the grand scheme of things, or what things are not of some grand scheme? Also, what about the main character or even sub-character(s); whose thoughts, speech, behavior, and looks, all of which either directly—or, indirectly affect—if not, effect the story's theme: or, better yet, effectuate such story's ending or the lack thereof. Some or even most short stories have some type of ending or a climatic resolution. However, it is not altogether un-heard of, for some short story or another short story to just end with a cliff-hanger, so to speak: to end climatically, or, not, and, with no real resolution. By chance, the author or the narrator just wants the reader to form his or her own content, and, creative, and even, critical conclusion.

What is more, to effectuate the short stories' various endings; I have chosen to construct or create certain effects with regard to the traditionally fictional essentials—or, fictional fundamentals...: point of view (*POV*); plot; characterization; theme; and the like, with-standing their eventual clashes, and, climaxes, and even, conclusions, so, respectively. Further, I have chosen to explore the traditional *POV's*—or, third person, editorial omniscient; and, third person, limited omniscient; and, even, objective. In "Part One," the protagonist—or, Zen, almost, certainly, speaks her mind. But, as omniscient author/narrator, I have so allowed, also, the antagonist's—or, Ben's thoughts and actions to be known or explored, to a great extent.

Perhaps, the very mixture of character traits or even qualities—actual, unique, representative, or otherwise; all of which can be so attributed to such character as Georgina, allows her, too, to have her thoughts and actions be explored or known. That, we are privy to know what the various characters think and all is the core of the omniscience. It is, as well, useful for you as an omni-present Reader to use your own content, and creative, and even critical-thinking skills; to refer, and draw some inferences, or some interpretations, if not some conclusions of your own, rightly, and autonomously. This is why, I, almost, always, insert independently objective; and, some-times, I just insert separately subjective questioning that is so aimed at you—the Reader, among other things.

Furthermore, that such characters speak their minds is the essence of exploring all of their minds and even conduct or the lack thereof. Zen's and Ben's struggles are separate, to a large extent. Yet, their circularly collective clash in the end is evitable, and, quite. They both arrive at such end by way of just letting go, and, more than ever, with the necessary help of a Muse of a God and even some other. The characters all just have to be strong, weak, or somewhere right in between, mentally, emotionally, and physically, and even spiritually.

On the whole, though, they are just life's highs and lows; or, ups and downs that move from side to side and back and forth easily and un-easily; right, along an un-steady pendulum of other states of conditions, with respect to rightness and/or wrongness and ethical or not. To have plotted a way to affect/effect a conclusion; for, this thematic thought of one needing not to be down propels Zen, at last, to just rise up: or, to perceive and believe and then achieve … whatever its cost.

At first, her perception may very well be that of one allowing one-self to be taken down and even held down. Because, of some wildly or woefully warped notion of duty and devotion. That, such references, or inferences, or even interpretations—and so forth, eventually, turns right into basic beliefs; plus, such serves, only, to then stifle Zen's unadulterated ability or capacity; rightly, to achieve her very full potential or deliciously if not decidedly good dreams. Likewise, and, largely, she almost certainly has to be smart, strong, and successful, among other things. Or, a circularly courageous stickler, who just sticks to that—which, almost, always, means the most: self-preservation, if not self-fulfillment, or even self-discovery.

In addition, in "Part Two," the point of view is far more limited than in part one. That is, we are restrained, essentially, from ever interpreting the thoughts and actions of the antagonist—Saul; or, his and Mable's daughter—Eva; or, even, some other sub-character's actions and thoughts…. Here, the protagonist—or, limiter—(or, even, very omniscient-limited author/narrator), or Mable does some interpreting. She so enlightens us, opening up her mind, heart, and, body, and, even, spirit. We, consequently, get an idea of what she thinks and feels about Saul. Plus, we even get an idea, subsequently, of what other sub-characters feel and think, as well as what motivate them to act or the lack thereof; all, right, through Mable's eyes, or interpreting.

She is aware, also, of the symbolic or allegorical or even metaphorical use of a very poisonous wild flower: *Harlequin Lupine (Lupinus stiversii)*—as, to affect if not effect her being or the lack thereof. That, such manages to materialize—and, almost, certainly, to personify, what Mable's struggle—or even clash, as it were, is all about: self-confidence, and self-control, plus self-preservation; all of which, can, almost, never, be about any self-mortification, or more precisely, self-destruction.

Because of some climatic confrontation—just, in a nick of time, she arises, absolutely, and roundly, to the overly onerous occasion. Mable wards off very smartly, and strongly, and even successfully, her nemeses: or, dark, deep, and dangerous powers or forces. Saul supposedly becomes some-what of a dark force, or power; or, Saul being vain, foolish, and, empty, among other things—quite possibly, unbeknown, to him. That he even un-knowingly plots his very own un-surprising down-fall, or defeat. Who, if any one could or would ever expect to win some self-defeating feat, deed?

Additionally, in "Part Three," the point of view is objective. This is to say, that the objective author/narrator is so restrained, most, essentially, from interpreting the thoughts and the actions of any character. Here, the authorial objector/narrator can only be so objectively descriptive; or, just, describe the behavior, speech, and looks, (minus any thoughts), of the characters or the lack thereof. The objective author/narrator can not and must not interpret anyone's thoughts, in any way, what so ever. Thus, you as Reader must use your own higher-order thinking skills, ultimately; and, rightly, to infer, refer, or interpret, and conclude what is truly in the minds, hearts, and bodies, and even souls of the characters.

Also, such inferences, references, interpretations, and conclusions—all, should take note of such characters' over-all existence. Their motivations, or purposes, whose purposeful or purposeless thoughts, words, actions, looks, and all, may or may not affect or effect the thematically climatic narrative: or, the story's ending, or, conclusion; all of which, ought to permit you—the Reader, to have your own bona-fide point-of-view (or *P.O.V.*)...: and, be it strong or weak, right or wrong, good or bad, or even some where in between, and so on.

Bear in mind—that, an objective point of view may very well afford you—the Reader, the most freedom...; as, in drawing your own references, inferences, plus, interpretations, and, even, conclusions, or, the lack thereof. However, it almost certainly affords you, as well, the objective opportunity; rightly, to validate, or even in-validate a short story or a long story—or, just, remain neutral in your conclusive interpretation of it, story. That is, you need not draw any autonomous references, inferences, or, interpretations, or, even, conclusions, at all. Rather, you may very well just accept some story as told by the narrator—or, the author, at its face value—and, with all it has or has not.

Finally, we are reminded that our own creative plus critical-thinking processes are highly imperative in as much as relevant; right, toward drawing an affective, if not an effective, or even an effectual conclusion so concerning a short story, (or any story…). Whether such story has a climatic close or a sound resolution may—or, may not be, beside the point. Yet, some thematic point(s) is/are almost, always, intrinsic, to a story either directly or indirectly. It is, once again, that some theme or topic can be just as important as a main character's, or a sub-character's views, words, and ways, and even looks, all; amid whatever else, that just so happens to be happening—right, in the grand scheme of things or the lack thereof. This brings us right back, in-escapably, and, so, fundamentally, to the essentials—or, the fundamentals: theme—but, of course, and characterization—whether actual, unique, or, representative, or otherwise, plot, story, setting, and the like.

Still, short, that it may very well be; yet, a short story ought not to lack those fundamentals or essentials, which are listed, right, above. Neither should a short story lack other typical but very important rudiments or basics: point of view, (or, one solid *POV*, most, typically), struggle, affect/effect, clash, climax, and, closing; all of which are almost always compressed and charged in one way or another way or even some other way. Likewise, what may very well be the most crucial thing of all: A short story almost certainly concerns it-self with only a single aware-ness; which is to say, that it almost never deals with more than one very concrete consciousness withstanding its complexity or even the lack thereof.